Bonnie wasn't thinking so much about Mark lately.

In fact, as she spent an hour getting ready, she found herself thinking more about concocting a reason to stop at *Dalton's* on her way out—once she was all dressed up. Which was how she finally settled on a red sleeveless cocktail dress that fit like a dream....

"You are smoking in that dress...." Dalton said. "This is your chance, right...? With Mark."

"Yes. That is what I was thinking," Bonnie said.

"Sweetheart, if you're dressed like that..." He gave a shake of his head. "This is your big night."

If she'd imagined, even for a moment, that Dalton wanted her for himself, this clinched it. He didn't. "You think so? For me and Mark?"

Three heartbeats passed between them....

Dear Reader,

We're deep into spring, and the season and romance always seem synonymous to me. So why not let your reading reflect that? Start with Sherryl Woods's next book in THE ROSE COTTAGE SISTERS miniseries, *The Laws of Attraction*. This time it's Ashley's turn to find love at the cottage—which the hotshot attorney promptly does, with a man who appears totally different from the cutthroat lawyers she usually associates with. But you know what they say about appearances....

Karen Rose Smith's *Cabin Fever* is the next book in our MONTANA MAVERICKS: GOLD RUSH GROOMS continuity, in which a handsome playboy and his beautiful secretary are hired to investigate the mine ownership issue. But they're snowbound in a cabin...and work can only kill so much time! And in *Lori's Little Secret* by Christine Rimmer, the next of her BRAVO FAMILY TIES stories, a young woman who was always the shy twin has a big secret (two, actually): seven years ago she pretended to be her more outgoing sister—which resulted in a night of passion and a baby, now child. And said child's father is back in town... Judy Duarte offers another of her BAYSIDE BACHELORS, in *Worth Fighting For*, in which a single adoptive mother—with the help of her handsome neighbor, who's dealing with a loss of his own—grapples with the possibility of losing her child. In Elizabeth Harbison's hilarious new novel, a young woman who wonders how to get her man finds help in a book entitled, well, *How To Get Your Man*. But she's a bit confused about which man she really wants to get! And in *His Baby to Love* by Karen Sandler, a long-recovered alcoholic needs to deal with her unexpected pregnancy, so she gratefully accepts her friend's offer of her chalet for the weekend. But she gets an unexpected roommate—the one man who'd pointed her toward recovery...and now has some recovering of his own to do.

So enjoy, and we'll see you next month, when things once again start to heat up, in Silhouette Special Edition!

Sincerely yours,

Gail Chasan
Senior Editor

Please address questions and book requests to:
Silhouette Reader Service
U.S.: 3010 Walden Ave., P.O. Box 1325, Buffalo, NY 14269
Canadian: P.O. Box 609, Fort Erie, Ont. L2A 5X3

HOW TO GET
YOUR MAN

ELIZABETH HARBISON

Silhouette

SPECIAL EDITION

Published by Silhouette Books

America's Publisher of Contemporary Romance

To Nancy Nesbit Preston
Cool Chick Extraordinaire

 SILHOUETTE BOOKS

ISBN 0-373-24685-4

HOW TO GET YOUR MAN

This edition published by arrangement with Harlequin Books S.A.

® and TM are trademarks of Harlequin Books S.A., used under license. Trademarks indicated with ® are registered in the United States Patent and Trademark Office, the Canadian Trade Marks Office and in other countries.

Visit Silhouette Books at www.eHarlequin.com

Printed in U.S.A.

Books by Elizabeth Harbison

Silhouette Special Edition

Drive Me Wild #1476
Midnight Cravings #1539
How To Get Your Man #1685

Silhouette Romance

A Groom for Maggie #1239
Wife without a Past #1258
Two Brothers and a Bride #1286
True Love Ranch #1323
Emma and the Earl #1410
Plain Jane Marries the Boss #1416
Annie and the Prince #1423
His Secret Heir #1528
A Pregnant Proposal #1553
Princess Takes a Holiday #1643
The Secret Princess #1713

*Cinderella Brides

Silhouette Books

Lone Star Country Club
Mission Creek Mother-To-Be

ELIZABETH HARBISON

has been an avid reader for as long as she can remember. After devouring the Nancy Drew and Trixie Belden series in grade school, she moved on to the suspense of Mary Stewart, Dorothy Eden and Daphne du Maurier, just to name a few. From there it was a natural progression to writing, although early efforts have been securely hidden away in the back of a closet.

After authoring three cookbooks, Elizabeth turned her hand to writing romances and hasn't looked back. Her second book for Silhouette Romance, *Wife Without a Past,* was a 1998 finalist for the Romance Writers of America's prestigious RITA® Award in the Best Traditional Romance category.

Elizabeth lives in Maryland with her husband, John, daughter Mary Paige, and son, Jack, as well as two dogs, Bailey and Zuzu. She loves to hear from readers and you can write to her c/o Box 1636, Germantown, MD 20875.

Fall 1980
INTERIM REPORT for Bonnie Jane Vaness
Tappen Elementary School—
Teacher: Dinah Perry—Grade 2

Bonnie is doing wonderfully academically. Her handwriting is coming along beautifully and she seems quite gifted in both English and science. She is very organized.

Unfortunately, Bonnie does need to exercise control socially. She sometimes talks in class with her friend Paul Czarny, and often bickers with classmate Dalton Price. I have separated the two of them on numerous occasions but they always end up together, arguing.

INTERIM REPORT for Dalton James Price
Tappen Elementary School—
Teacher: Dinah Perry—Grade 2

Dalton is a spirited child. He is very capable, but seems to have trouble applying himself. He'd rather pick on his classmate, Bonnie Vaness, than pay attention to the lessons. Though I separate the two of them, they somehow seem to manage to find each other again....

Prologue

"*...Our guest today is Leticia Bancroft, author of the controversial book,* How To Seduce Your Dream Man. *Leticia, tell me about the reception your book has gotten.*"

"It's setting women back fifty years," Bonnie Vaness said to the television, dabbing her sore, red nose with a tissue. "Of course it's getting a great reception." She threw the covers back to look for the television remote, but only found more tissues. It seemed like every November she got a raging cold just before Thanksgiving, and this year was no exception.

She must have been through at least four boxes of tissue in the past three days.

"As far as I'm concerned," Leticia said, *"the reaction to the book has been fantastic. But don't take my word for it. Let's talk to some of the women in the audience."*

The audience erupted into applause.

Bonnie cursed and moved the pillows aside searching for the remote.

"Honestly, I didn't think it was going to work," a woman who actually looked normal was saying. In fact, she even looked a little embarrassed to be talking into the microphone.

Bonnie stopped her search and looked at the TV.

"When I first heard about the book, I was a little offended. I figured it would set women back fifty years—"

"Exactly!" Bonnie cried, pointing at the screen.

"—but, then again, laying it all on the line wasn't getting me very far either. So I decided to read Leticia's book. I put on a disguise and went to a bookstore in another town and bought it." The audience chuckled.

Bonnie sneezed.

"I had a really bad romantic history. Lots of boyfriends, lots of breakups. I sometimes felt like I

couldn't find the kind of guy I really wanted, so I'd have to settle for less. But then I found the guy. And he didn't even know I existed."

Bonnie sat up and listened. This woman could be her. String of lousy boyfriends, equally long string of lousy breakups, fear that she'd have to lower her standards or end up alone, and then—this was the kicker—finding the man of her dreams only to have him be completely oblivious to her.

"But this book…" The woman paused, her voice filled with emotion. *"This book gave me ideas for getting his attention that I could use immediately. Actual, you know, techniques. Not a lot of academic philosophizing. Before I knew it, the man who hadn't known I was alive for six months was asking me out."*

"Tell them the rest," Leticia interjected excitedly, then turned to the hostess. *"You're going to love this."*

Bonnie sniffled and moved forward to hear better.

The woman held up her left hand, displaying a glittering stone the size of a cupcake. *"We're getting married next month!"*

The audience squealed with delight and erupted into applause again.

Bonnie wrote down the name of the book.

Chapter One

Men are very visual creatures. Discover his favorite colors and swathe yourself in them. This will make you a soothing, comfortable presence to him, though he won't realize exactly why. This is the first step in our Plan of Seduction.

Remember, color is very powerful and, just as you want to wear his favorites, you must avoid those he doesn't like. An unpleasant association with a color you wear can make you someone to avoid, rather than someone to adore.

—Leticia Bancroft, *How To Seduce Your Dream Man*

"Joining the army or something?"

Bonnie Vaness stopped in the middle of locking the dead bolt of her apartment and glanced impatiently behind her at Dalton Price, the building manager. "What are you talking about?"

"That outfit you've got on. It's the third ugly green thing you've worn this week."

Bonnie automatically put a hand to the new olive-green suit she'd gotten from Delaney's Department Store over on Quince Street. It had cost half a week's paycheck.

"Not that you wouldn't make a great soldier," he went on, raking a hand through black hair. "Temper like yours…"

"Shut up, Dalton."

He laughed. "Hey, I'm just saying—"

"I know what you're saying. You're saying I look horrible in this. Thanks."

He gave a broad shrug. "Now did I say that? I didn't say that. It's not you, it's the outfit. I'd think you'd be glad for the objective opinion, before you go trotting off into the world looking like that."

She didn't look at him. She didn't want him to see he was plucking away at her raw nerves like a bad street musician on a broken banjo.

Of course, Dalton Price had been plucking at Bonnie's nerves since second grade at Tappen Elementary School in Tappen, New Jersey, when he'd been the only one close enough to hear her accidentally call Mrs. Perry "Mommy." He'd spent years tormenting her about that and every other stupid thing she was unfortunate enough to do in his presence. His imagination was limitless.

"Don't you have something better to do than critique my clothing?" she asked him, uncomfortably aware that he might be right about the outfit. When she'd tried it on, she told herself the greenish tint to her face was from the fluorescent lighting in the dressing room, but now she was starting to think it was the reflected olive green bouncing off her skin.

She wasn't about to let Dalton know of her doubts.

"Isn't there a hairy sink waiting for you somewhere around here?" She clicked the lock in place and turned to face him.

Though she said it lightly, her curiosity about his job had been piqued for some time now. Ten years ago, Dalton had gotten a football scholarship to some college out west and everyone in town was abuzz about what a success he'd made of his life, and how he'd become an investment banker and married an actress from some since-canceled sitcom. Then, about four months ago, Dalton was suddenly back, divorced and with a nearly adolescent daughter in tow. Stranger still, despite his proximity to New York City, he wasn't working as an investment banker. He was working as a super in what was a nice old building but certainly not fancy.

Bonnie wondered if he'd ever really been successful or if that was his mother's fantasy.

At first she'd been sympathetic toward him, but he hadn't been in town two days before he started giving her the same old guff he'd always given her. And she gave it right back.

Some things never changed.

He leveled a blue-eyed gaze at her now. A gaze which had, she knew, reduced many foolish women to quivering puddles of submission.

It only ticked Bonnie off.

"I fix everything that needs to be fixed," he said, in answer to her question.

"Yeah?" She dropped her keys in her bag. "Then fix my shower. It's been dripping since Carter was president."

"Carter who?"

Bonnie's mouth dropped open just as Dalton gave a sly smile.

"Man, you're such a sucker," he said.

"I am not, I just…" She stopped. Yes, she was. He'd suckered her over and over. Someday she'd learn.

"Don't you have a bus to catch?" he asked her, interrupting her private reverie.

"Oh! Yes." Why did she find Dalton's presence so disconcerting? "Paula's waiting downstairs and she'll kill me if we miss the bus into town because I had to stop and fight with you again."

He smiled and slipped a wrench out of his back pocket. "I'll be around later. You can yell at me then. Meantime, I'm gonna go fix Mrs. Neuhouse's leaky faucet."

"And my shower…?"

"It's on the list," he said over his shoulder as he walked away.

"I'd like to see this list."

"Come by later tonight." He didn't look back. "I'll show it to you. It's under my pillow."

It was hard to believe he got women with that kind of line. Bonnie figured there were a lot of girls out there who were so blown away by his looks that they didn't care about anything else. Idiots. "Just fix the shower, all right?"

"Daddy!" A young girl with pale gold hair came running around the corner. "Wait! Daddy!"

Elissa. His nine-year-old daughter.

Bonnie paused and watched the two of them together. She couldn't help it. Not only was she enchanted by the girl—she had been ever since she'd first laid eyes on her—but she was also captivated by the sweet interaction between father and daughter. Bonnie's own father had passed away in a car accident before she was old enough to know him, and she had always had a soft spot for good father-daughter relationships.

For all Dalton Price's faults, even Bonnie approved of his parenting.

"I thought Mrs. Malone took you to school already," he said to his daughter, with that tenderness that never failed to tug at Bonnie's heart.

Nelly Malone was an elderly neighbor who lived in the building. She was practically like a grandmother to Elissa and loved to spend time with her. Bonnie sometimes wondered if Elissa was doing more for Nelly than the other way around.

"I forgot my lunch money again," Elissa told Dalton.

"Ah, okay." He reached into his pocket for his wallet and pulled out a single. "That enough?"

"*Daddy,* it's a dollar sixty just for lunch. You know that. *And* dessert is extra." She shook her head but smiled. "We should just set up an account at the school like all the other kids do."

"You don't need to start living on credit this early." He took out another two dollars, handed them to her and ruffled her hair. "Here you go, baby. Get an ice-cream sandwich for dessert. I love those things."

"Okay! Thanks!" She threw her arms around him and hugged him before clambering down the stairs like a toy that had been wound up in his hands.

With an ache in her chest, Bonnie watched her go, then watched Dalton sigh, shake his head slightly, and go up the stairs toward Mrs. Neuhouse's apartment.

Five minutes later she and Paula Czarny walked down the chipped sidewalk of Tappen Avenue toward the bus that took them to Hoboken, where they took a ferry into Manhattan every morning. It was a balmy fall morning, close to seventy degrees but in the sun it felt warmer. Bonnie was already sweating in her suit.

"So tell me why you're wearing this horrible drab color all the time lately, even though it's hideous and makes you look like you're seasick," Paula said.

"You don't like it either?"

"Hate it." She frowned and looked at Bonnie. "What do you mean 'either?'"

Bonnie gave an exasperated groan. "Dalton Price. Couldn't let me leave today without giving me at least one thing to feel self-conscious about. God, I hate him sometimes."

"I think he's hot."

This made Bonnie impatient. "You've always had lousy taste in men."

Paula shrugged. "At least we'll never fight over one. So, seriously, about this outfit. And the silk one yesterday. Is this what you're doing with all the money you get from that fancy ad agency? Buying the most hideous clothes you can find?"

Bonnie sighed. It wasn't her first choice in colors either, but she had a mission. She'd bought these clothes with the single purpose of winning over Mark Ford, the new vice president of marketing at her company. He'd started working there four months ago and Bonnie had been…intrigued…ever since.

He was the kind of guy you saw in cologne commercials, gliding across a sea of blue glass in a big white sailboat, his dark blond hair mussed by the wind, his face kissed golden by the sun. He was a modern Prince Charming whose smile promised a lifetime of happily ever after.

Bonnie wanted a lifetime of happily ever after.

"You're missing the big picture here." Bonnie stepped gingerly over a pile of what she hoped was only mud. "The *reason* I'm wearing this color is because Mark Ford *likes* this color. No, he *loves* this color. His entire office is painted this color."

Paula stopped and gave her friend a look that mingled disbelief and disapproval. "And you want to look like his office. This is your grand scheme to seduce him, to blend into the walls of his *workplace*."

Bonnie shook her head. It did sound stupid, put that way. "Leticia Bancroft says men have a powerful subconscious reaction to color. Wear a color he likes and he'll be drawn to you like…" She searched for the perfect analogy but came up short. "A magnet. A really strong magnet."

They started walking again and Paula stepped squarely in what Bonnie was now fairly certain *wasn't* mud, muttered an oath and scraped the stiletto heel of her shoe on the curb before saying, "I don't think you ought to want a man who loves drab green." She finished scraping her shoe and they resumed their walk down the hill toward the bus stop. "Sounds like some sort of latent militia thing to me. Like those guys out in the Midwest. Is it the Midwest? Or the Northwest?"

"He is *not* the militia type," Bonnie said, increasing her gait. She didn't want to miss the bus again. She had a meeting at ten with, among others, Mark, and she did not want to come in late, soaked in sweat from running to Hoboken to catch the ferry to lower

Manhattan. "He's the blond, blue-eyed, captain of the football team type. The weekend house in the Hamptons type." Definitely *not* the type to sneak into a closet with another woman at the office Christmas party; probably not the type to pass out on the front sidewalk after a night out with the guys; and absolutely not the type to fixate on buxom young blondes. No, Mark Ford was a grown-up. It was about time Bonnie went out with a grown-up. She would have sighed longingly if she weren't running. "The marry-me-and-father-my-children type."

"Sounds dull."

Bonnie looked at her. "It's not dull. It's mature. Logical instead of just chemical. Unlike this thing you have for *Mister* Parker…." Mr. Parker was Paula's boss. His first name was Seamus, but Paula thought it was "sexier" to call him Mr. Parker. "Or are you trying to tell me that's love?"

"No way, baby, that's *lust.* Good ol' lust. Oh, crud, there goes the bus!"

Bonnie looked up just as the bus rumbled away from the curb at the bottom of Tappen Avenue.

"Hey!" Paula shouted, pulling her shoes off so she could run faster. "Hey, wait a minute!"

Bonnie, in more sensible, though olive-green, shoes, pounded down the sidewalk after her.

Paula shouted an expletive and the bus jerked to a halt and the door shuddered open.

Bonnie caught a glimpse of an old woman in a scarf looking out the window, and she winced. "Paula, have a little respect."

"You're such a goody two-shoes," Paula said to her, climbing the steps. "Seven-forty," she snapped at the driver when she reached him. "This bus isn't supposed to leave until seven-*forty*. It is now—" she thrust her wristwatch in front of the driver's face "—seven thirty-seven. Thanks to you, I've probably got runs in my stockings and I'm gonna look hideous when I get to work."

"I didn't tell you to run around widout your shoes on," the driver said in a thick Jersey accent.

He couldn't have been more than twenty or twenty-one, Bonnie thought. He had no idea what he was up against. She'd known Paula since kindergarten and she'd never known her to let go of an argument until some sort of blood was spilled. Hopefully humiliation and an abject apology would suffice.

Paula drew up her petite frame. "The West Hudson County transit authority, who issues your paychecks by the way, employs you to follow the schedule that they've set forth. When you drive away before your appointed pickup time, you are, in fact, breaking your employment contract. Which is grounds for termination." She narrowed her eyes at the driver. "Which means you'd be sacked. Got it?" She rifled through her large handbag and pulled out a pad of paper and a pen. "Now what's your name?"

"Don Vittoni," he said miserably.

She wrote and said, "Okay, listen, Don Vittoni, I'll let it slide this time, but if you do it again, I'm gonna have to write a letter to your boss. Got it?"

He nodded.

"Good." She smiled and turned to Bonnie, who was now cringing with embarrassment as the entire bus had gone quiet. "Let's find some seats."

Three men scrambled to their feet, vacating their seats.

"Thank you, gentlemen," Paula said sweetly, pulling Bonnie down the aisle with her.

They sat and the bus thundered away from the curb. Paula tapped the face of her watch. "Seven-forty. Right on schedule."

"I think poor Don Vittoni nearly wet himself," Bonnie commented as they rumbled down the rough road toward the city.

"That'll teach him. Now, where were we?"

"When?"

"Oh, yes, green—"

"Do we have to talk about this?"

"—it's not slimming, you know."

"What are you saying, I look fat in this?"

"Well…yeah. Not that I think you should lose weight or anything."

"Really?" Hope surged. For as long as she could remember, Bonnie had been ten pounds over the insurance chart weights for her height.

"Yeah. I think you'd look weird skinny."

Bonnie's heart sank.

"I just think, you know, you should wear clothes that flatter you," Paula said. "Like black."

"Because it's slimming?" Bonnie glared at Paula. It wasn't the first time she'd called attention to the extra padding Bonnie carried around with her. She'd been doing it since seventh grade. And all that time, Paula had stayed infuriatingly thin, with a tiny waist and the kind of heart-shaped butt that men loved.

"No, because with that pale blond hair of yours it's really striking. Red, too. And red would give your cheeks a little color."

"God, now I'm pale. Look, Paula, I have a meeting with Mark this morning. This is just the kind of pep talk I *don't* need, all right?"

Paula raised her hands. "All right, all right, I'm just trying to help."

"Well, you're not."

"Okay. I won't say another word." Paula pantomimed locking her lips and throwing away the key.

"Good."

A split second of silence passed.

"Except to say this: if you want to seduce this guy, you ought to throw away that book and use your brain instead. Men like sex."

Several heads swiveled their way.

"Am I wrong?" Paula asked the elderly gentleman next to her. "Men like sex, right? They like to see a little skin."

Bonnie's face burned.

The elderly woman sitting next to the elderly man leaned toward Paula and said, "They certainly do."

Paula splayed her arms. "*Thank* you." She turned to Bonnie with a smug expression. "There, see? I told you."

"Very scientific."

"Ask anyone here." Paula started to stand up but Bonnie grabbed her and hauled her back down again. There was a guy several seats down dressed as what appeared to be a Power Ranger. Bonnie did *not* want to engage him in a conversation about sex.

"Stop it!" she said to Paula. "Look, you do things your way and I'll do things mine."

"Okay, but I'll bet you I get my boss before you get yours."

"He's not exactly my boss, he's the vice president of the company. But your point is taken. And you're wrong."

"So we have a bet?" Paula held out her hand. "Whoever gets her dream man first wins dinner at Martini's."

"Will it shut you up?"

"For now."

Bonnie put her hand out. "Then it's a deal."

By four o'clock in the afternoon, Mark Ford had postponed his meeting with Bonnie two times. She was beginning to think it wasn't going to happen when his administrative assistant called hers at four-fifteen and asked if she could go to his office.

It took only about ten minutes for them to agree on their handling of a new account, but during that time Bonnie noticed he kept solid eye contact with her. That was a good thing. Leticia Bancroft had mentioned eye contact as a major key to seduction.

Bonnie was collecting her notes when Mark suddenly said, "Hey, can I ask you something a little…off topic?" He gave her a dazzling smile.

Wow—could Leticia Bancroft's advice really be working this fast? "Sure."

"Do you know anyone here who might be willing to spend a little overtime with me? I need some help getting my office into shape—" he glanced around and lowered his voice "—for obvious reasons."

Obvious? What did that mean? Was he being coy? Was this his way of asking her if she'd be willing to see him after hours? She knew better than to assume and make a fool of herself. "What did you have in mind?" she asked, hoping that was generic enough to be an appropriate and encouraging response to any of several things he might be alluding to.

She wished Leticia Bancroft were here to interpret his body language because Bonnie was lost.

"Well, it's this paint." He leaned forward and said conspiratorially, "When Brian asked if I wanted army green, I thought he was joking." He made a face. "I mean, come on, who would want to look at this color all day? It's depressing."

Bonnie couldn't have been more aware of her own suit at that moment if it had been on fire. "I see…" she hedged.

"So I was thinking maybe I'd just pick something else—*anything* else, really—and ask maintenance to handle it in the evening. So it's not so obvious to Brian that I'm changing it so soon."

She nodded. "So you need someone to pick out paint?"

"Exactly. Paint and accent pieces. Make the place look modern." He gave another winning grin. "Make me look like a power player."

Something inside of her softened, despite her embarrassment at being swathed in a color it was now obvious he detested. He hadn't meant to offend her, of course. He had no idea she wore the color to lure him. And now he was revealing a little bit of good old-fashioned humility and insecurity. That was good. She'd never dated a man who was willing to open up.

"I'd be glad to help you."

"Really? I'd hate to bother you with this." He glanced at her suit, perhaps doubtful of her ability to pick colors.

Would he? Was he really just in this for the paint?

"If there's an administrative assistant who might have more free time…" he went on, giving her a questioning look.

What did *that* mean?

It only took her a split second to decide it didn't matter what he meant, because she'd already volunteered to help him and even if he was giving her an out, she'd look like a jerk for taking it.

"Honestly, I don't mind helping you out. It would be a nice change of pace."

"Great. Thanks a million."

"It's nothing. When do you want to go?" She'd gone one step too far. She knew it as soon as the words left her lips. "I'm free tonight."

He shook his head. "I can't make it tonight—"

She shouldn't have said it. She *knew* she shouldn't have said it. Pages twenty-one through twenty-five of the book went on at great length about *not* pressing the man for a date but letting him make all the moves.

"But if you want to go get some ideas and bring them in tomorrow, that'd be super."

What could she do? She couldn't say she was suddenly unavailable. So she nodded. "No problem."

"Maybe you can show me what you come up with over lunch tomorrow."

"Sorry, I can't make lunch tomorrow." This was really counterintuitive. He was asking her out, that's what she wanted, so how did it make sense to say no? It didn't. This was a science, not a game. "How about Wednesday?" she suggested, feeling Leticia Bancroft's figurative ruler on her knuckles again.

He looked at his desk calendar and made a quick note. "Wednesday it is. I've got you down."

"Wonderful." She smiled. "I'll see you on Wednesday then."

It wasn't until she left his office and closed the door behind her that she finally thought about what had just happened.

She had a date with Mark Ford. A lunch date, granted, but it was still a date. Technically.

This was progress.

Chapter Two

The key to making a man fall in love with you is making him feel comfortable around you. One of the best ways to achieve this is by a little technique I like to call "mirror breathing."

Next time you're together, watch his breathing pattern and match yours to his. When he breathes in, you breathe in. When he breathes out, you breathe out. This sends a subconscious signal to the man that you are on the same frequency and that, thus, you are a safe person to open up to.

The results will amaze you.
—Leticia Bancroft, *How To Seduce Your*
                              Dream Man

It was just bad luck to run into Dalton Price at the Tappen Home Center that night.

"The building has approved colors if you're planning to redecorate, you know." He nodded at the handful of paint samples she was holding.

"These aren't for me." She paused and looked at him. "*Approved* colors? You've got to be kidding."

"Yup." They edged toward the long checkout line. "I am. You can paint the whole damn building pink if you want."

"Gee, thanks. Then you get paid for my work, huh?"

"You always think the worst of me, don't you, Bon?"

"That doesn't seem to bother you."

He grinned. "Nah. I know you're just fighting an attraction to me."

With that smile, he could almost be right. But Bonnie had already fought her attraction to him, and won. A long, long time ago.

"So, what are you doing here?" she asked, watching him put a collection of screwdriver bits, some duct tape and a fancy new showerhead on the conveyer belt. "I suppose I shouldn't dare to hope that's to fix my shower."

"Actually—" he handed a platinum credit card to the cashier "—it is."

She raised her eyebrows. "Really?"

He nodded.

"Gosh, the landlord's getting generous."

He hesitated, then signed the charge slip and took his bags. "The building's changing hands. I guess the new owner wants to make a better impression than the last guy."

"Hm. As long as he doesn't want to make a lot more money than the last guy, we'll be all right. And as long as he doesn't make too many changes." She'd lived in the old building for five years now, ever since she'd graduated from college and come back to Tappen. She loved the place. Loved its old fixtures, glass doorknobs, carved wooden doors and clanging fire escapes. Sure, everything needed work, but she hoped to heaven the place hadn't been bought by some upstart who wanted to turn it into one of those generic boxes that were springing up all over the suburbs.

"I don't think you've got to worry," Dalton said as they stepped into the crisp evening air outside the Home Center.

She shrugged. "I hope not."

He indicated a beat-up Toyota parked in front of the store. "So, you want a ride back?"

"No, thanks, I can use the walk."

"Eight blocks? With your arms full like that? Come on, Bon. It's cold out here."

A cold front had moved in, and it was crisp, even for November. "Don't worry about me." She opened her purse to stuff the paint samples in but lost her grip on the strap and the whole thing dropped to the ground.

How To Seduce Your Dream Man was, of course, the first thing to plunk out onto the sidewalk.

"Let me help you." Dalton bent down to help gather the things that had spilled.

"No—"

But it was too late. He took the book in hand and stood up.

"How to seduce your dream man?" He looked at the book, then at Bonnie, incredulous. "You've got to be kidding."

Her cheeks flamed. "It's not *mine*. It's for a campaign I'm working on." She snatched the book away from him and shoved it into her purse, not caring what she bent, broke or shattered in doing so, just as long as it was out of sight.

"A campaign."

"Yes. For a very important client."

"Hm." He went to his car and opened the back

door, saying over his shoulder, "Hell, *I* could tell you a hundred ways to get a guy right now. For the sake of your client, I mean."

"Like…?"

He put his bags on the seat, shut the door and came back to her. "Like stop dressing like an old lady."

"Me?"

He moved fractionally closer and she felt his warmth move into her space. "Yeah, you." He reached over to undo her top two buttons. His fingertips brushed against her skin, leaving a small trail of tingles after his touch.

Her breath caught in her throat and for just a split second she felt like a blushing teenager.

She stepped back. "Keep your hands off me!"

He gave a laugh. "You've been saying that since high school. Loosen up a little."

She swallowed hard, still reeling from her reaction to his touch more than his impertinence. "*You've* been saying *that* since high school."

He gave a rakish grin. "But I meant something different back then. Back then I was just trying to help *me*. Now I'm trying to help *you*."

"I think you even said *that* in high school."

He clicked his tongue against his teeth. "Man, if I'd known you were actually listening to what I was saying, I would have been a lot more careful."

"You probably should have been anyway." She wondered if he remembered the one single night they'd spent together as well as she did. She wondered if he knew it had been her first time and that when he hadn't called her back, it had made her feel cheap and tawdry.

"I'm going," she said, taking a step away. "See you later."

He watched her for a moment, frowning. "What did I say?"

"Nothing." She wasn't about to admit she was still holding on to a hurt that he'd inflicted eleven years ago. "I just want to get walking."

"Bon—" He came up behind her and took her by the arm, turning her to face him. "What's wrong?" His face was serious, still. Handsome in the twilight.

"Dalton, nothing's wrong. Can't a girl get some exercise if she wants to? It's a nice night, I just want to walk."

He studied her for a moment and she stood still under his scrutiny. "If that's all it is."

"That's all it is," she assured him.

"Because I didn't mean to say anything that would hurt you."

It wouldn't be fair to make the man pay for a mistake the boy had made so long ago. She gave a smile. "Careful, Dalton. Someone might think you care."

His blue eyes narrowed, tweaking laugh lines she hadn't noticed for a long time. "Does someone actually think I don't?"

Her throat went tight. So did her chest. That he could elicit this kind of response from her troubled her more than anything else. "Don't go soft on me."

He shook his head, a smile denting his cheek. "I'd never do that."

Well, she'd set herself up for that one. "Go home, Dalton." She turned and walked away, feeling his eyes on her back until she finally heard his car rumble to life and drive past her.

Only then did she relax.

The next day, Bonnie discovered that Leticia Bancroft's mirror-breathing technique was a disaster.

Bonnie had never realized before just how hard it was to breathe consciously. In when Mark breathed in, out when he exhaled. It took so much concentration, she could barely think about anything else.

Maybe if they'd been lying quietly in bed—a scenario she liked—she could have done it, but with him sitting at a table in front of her, moving every once in awhile to get papers or artwork or whatever, she couldn't keep up.

When he eventually looked at her and asked if she

was hyperventilating—his hand hovering over the telephone, ready to call for help—she decided to give up.

"It was so embarrassing," she said to Paula later that night at Bungalow Billiards, a little dive of a bar in Tappen. "The idea, as I understood it, was that this was supposed to create a *sub*conscious feeling of comfort in him. It wasn't supposed to make me look ill."

Paula downed a big gulp of beer. "Frankly I think all of this makes you look ill. Think about it, you're reading a book on how to make a man fall in love with you!"

Bonnie squeezed a slice of lime into her club soda. "I've been back here for five years, working five days a week in a bustling metropolis that you would *think* would have men to spare, yet I've met no one interesting. Mark is the first guy I've really thought might be It. I mean, if you look at his stats, he's perfect for me." She shrugged. "I've got to do what I can."

"His stats? What about chemistry?"

Bonnie shook her head. "Oh, no, no, no, chemistry has failed me far too often. I'm not listening to that anymore. I'm listening to my head on this one, and my head tells me Mark is perfect for me."

Paula looked skeptical. "Then I think you ought

to consider Dalton's offer. Get a real guy's take on seduction, not some highfalutin semi-psychologist's."

"For one thing, Dalton wasn't really *offering* anything except snide commentary. And for another thing, I stopped trusting Dalton Price's judgment a long time ago."

"He's a guy. You can't argue with that."

"No. I can't."

"A guy who knows women."

"Tons of them."

"That makes him an expert in my book."

"Well, in my book, that makes him something else." She took a sip of soda. "Look, Bancroft has got the numbers behind her. I looked at her Web site. Over a thousand women have reported marriage proposals that they attribute *directly* to her book, and that's just over the past three months. She's onto something."

"I'll say," a familiar voice said from behind her. "She knows how to make money off of desperate women."

Paula stifled a laugh and Bonnie turned around. "Dalton. How nice to see you again."

He signaled the bartender for a beer and said to Bonnie, "So that book was for a client, huh?"

Her face warmed. "One of my favorites."

He smiled. "Mine, too. Come on, Bon. You like a guy, he likes you, what's the problem? Be yourself. Why use tricks?"

"Because the guy doesn't know she exists," Paula interjected.

Bonnie shot her a look before turning back to Dalton. "Maybe not, but he will soon."

"If a guy doesn't know you exist, he's got to be blind." Dalton took the beer the bartender handed him, sloshing some over the side and onto the scarred wooden bar top.

Bonnie flushed at his compliment. Why did he affect her this way? This was *Dalton Price,* for crying out loud. "From your lips—"

"Speaking of lips," he said, pulling up a bar stool and sitting uncomfortably close to her. "What's with the red lipstick?"

Red lips remind men, on a primal level, of the fruit of your sex, ripe for the picking.—Leticia Bancroft.

"Nothing," Bonnie said.

"In the book, huh?"

She didn't answer.

A drunk swaggered up and asked Paula to dance. She accepted and bounced out to the dance floor, leaving Dalton and Bonnie alone.

"Look, I need to talk to you about something

else," Dalton said, dragging the basket of pretzels closer to him. "I need a favor."

"Did you fix my shower?"

"I did."

She smiled. "Okay, shoot."

"You know how I told you the building had a new owner?"

She nodded.

"Yeah, well, it's me."

Her mouth dropped open. "You? You bought the building?" She thought of Elissa, and her future security, and felt a warm ember of pride in her chest.

"You don't need to sound so surprised. It wasn't like I just wanted to clean it up for someone else for the rest of my life. I was checking the place out."

"But how did you swing it? That place must have cost a fortune!"

He looked a little taken aback. "I've got some resources."

Bonnie could have kicked herself. She really needed to be more careful and think before speaking. "Of course you do, I didn't mean—"

"Whatever. Here's the thing. I want to fix the place up and get some advertising going. We only have sixty percent occupancy at the moment."

"I kind of like the emptiness."

He shook his head. "Much as I'd like to please you, I'd prefer to have more renters."

"Of course," she acknowledged. "But what can I do? I'm no Realtor."

"You're in advertising. You're surrounded by people who spend their lives making things look appealing to the public."

She was glad he didn't add a codicil about the exception of herself in drab green clothes and red lipstick. "True. But real estate…" She shook her head. "If you wanted to sell toothpaste, I'm a pro."

"I'll keep it in mind. Meantime, can you recommend someone who might want to take on some freelance ad work?"

So he wasn't even asking her to do it? "Someone else? Not me?"

He drank some beer and swiped the back of his hand across his mouth. "Is that what you thought? I was asking you to do it?"

She took a pretzel from the basket in front of him. "What are you saying, you don't trust me to do it?"

"You just said you can only sell toothpaste."

"I didn't say I could *only* sell toothpaste. All I meant was, yours is a different job than I'm used to doing."

He shrugged. "And you don't feel capable of handling it on your own. I get that."

"Hey, it's not rocket science. I think I could handle it."

"Yeah? Hey, thanks for offering." He gave a broad smile. "I'll take you up on that."

Once again, Dalton had steered the conversation to his benefit. "Wait a minute, I didn't mean—" She couldn't give him this. "What's in it for me?"

"I could pay you, of course. Or—" he smiled "—we could barter."

"Barter?"

He nodded. "I help you get your guy."

Her face went hot. It felt like far too many people knew about her quest for—and inability to get—Mark Ford. "Seriously, Dalton."

"I *am* serious. Money has a finite value, but the wisdom of experience…" He tapped his temple with his index finger. "Priceless. I can unlock the secrets of seduction for you."

She gave him a skeptical look. "I'm not interested in hands-on training, you know."

"There's no better way to learn."

She scoffed and started to turn away. "Thanks, but no thanks."

He stopped her. "But first things first. You need the basics."

"Now you're saying I don't even have the basics?"

"Oh, you've got 'em all right. You're just not using them. You're going about this all wrong."

"Meaning…?"

"The lipstick, the ugly clothes. Forget it. If you really want this undeserving slob, I can help you get him." He shrugged. "Or I could pay you and you could go out and burn more bucks on bad advice. Whatever you want."

She wanted Mark. And she had to admit that the Bancroft method wasn't really going all that well.

But what if Dalton was wrong, too? He knew how to get women, God knew, but that didn't automatically mean he knew how women could get men. Men like him, maybe, but a guy like Mark Ford? Maybe she was better off sticking with the advice of an expert like Leticia Bancroft.

"I'll think about it," she said.

Dalton raked a hand through his wavy dark hair. His eyes were bright with amusement. "You don't think I can help you."

"What?"

He'd always, always, *always* been able to read her. It drove her absolutely nuts.

"I wasn't born with blue blood so you don't think I can help you get some guy who was."

She did think that. "No, I don't."

He laughed outright. "Sure you do. You also think you have to be Miss Park Avenue 2005 in order to snag a guy who's gainfully employed in midtown, which would explain your recent change of wardrobe." He looked her up and down. "This guy work in your building?"

"That doesn't make any difference."

"So he does. I knew it. I bet he went to one of those fancy Ivy League schools too, right?"

After a moment of contemplating denial, she nodded.

"That's why you've got this preppy look going on. You believe you need to look like the girls he's been around all his life. And like everything you believe, you're going to have a hell of a time letting go of that idea."

"See, this is exactly why you can't help me," Bonnie said, trying to deflect some of the attention from herself and how right he was about her. "You always think you know better than I do."

"I usually do."

"Not this time."

"Okay." He gave a broad shrug. "Do it your way. This should be fun. I can't wait to see what you come up with next. Vanilla perfume to make him think of Mom? Feathers in your hair to make him feel free?" He downed his beer and started to walk away.

Studies show that men react to the scents of vanilla and pumpkin pie. Try to incorporate those scents subtly into your environment, to make him relax.—Leticia Bancroft.

"Wait," Bonnie called.

He stopped and turned around. "Yeah?"

"Are you a betting man?"

He gave a lazy smile and leaned against the bar. "What do you have in mind?"

She nodded toward the pool tables. "One game. If I win, I get—" she considered "—one month's rent free."

He looked skeptical. "And if I win?"

"I'll try this seduction thing your way."

He scoffed. "Sounds like I'm doing the work either way. And you win either way." He shook his head. "Thanks, but no thanks."

"Oh, okay, okay, if you win we'll do it your way *and* I'll create an ad campaign of some sort for you."

He considered this. "Far as I'm concerned, that's an even trade, not a winning bet."

She sighed. He was smarter than the average Tappen guy. Always had been. "So what else do you want?"

He thought for a moment, then a smile curved his lips. "As I recall, you were a pretty good cook."

She frowned. "And?"

"And I like to eat. So does Elissa." He tossed a pretzel in the air and caught it in his mouth. "So how about this: add five meals, my call, and you've got a deal."

"And if I win I get two months' rent free."

"One."

"One and a half."

"One."

He'd wear her down, she knew it. That was how she'd lost her virginity to him. "Okay. Deal."

"And you can't deviate from my plan to get your guy. You've got to do everything I say."

"Within reason." Something tremored through her. Excitement at the possibility of winning over Mark Ford? Reluctance to take the advice of a guy who had, himself, broken her heart? She honestly couldn't say.

"Honey, I'm always reasonable."

There was that tremor again.

They went to the vacant pool table by the window and Dalton racked the balls while Bonnie took out a cue and chalked the tip.

Dalton turned and watched her for a moment. "Not so hard. You're gonna break something."

She looked at the chalk, which was falling in crumbles to the ground. He was making her nervous, that was all. She blew the residue off the top of the cue and set the chalk down.

"Consider that your first lesson," Dalton said devilishly.

"In—" She realized what he meant. "Oh, jeez, Dalton. Keep your mind out of the gutter."

"And you get off your high horse." He stepped back and gestured for her to break. "Consider that lesson two. A little gutter thinking could only help your cause."

"There's a difference between sex and the gutter, you know."

His smile was sly. "It's a fine line."

He was kidding, and it was obnoxious, but she was struck by how sexy he still was. Suddenly she remembered what it felt like to fall for Dalton. She recalled the feeling of being with him in the back seat of his old Chevy Impala, remembered the feel of his muscular body, the taste of him, the smell of him. After eleven years the memory should have faded, but it hadn't.

Eager to push the thoughts aside, she bent over the table and broke the balls with a loud *crack*. The heavy balls scattered, bouncing off the velvet walls of the table. The cue ball jumped the side and dropped heavily onto the floor.

Dalton looked at the cue ball for a moment, then calmly bent over, picked it up and set it on the table.

"Something on your mind?" he asked, straight-faced.

"I think it's your turn."

He laughed and dropped two striped balls into pockets before scratching. Bonnie took a cleansing breath and made one clean shot, six ball into the corner pocket.

After that, her game improved considerably and for a good half she was ahead. She was already counting the money she'd save with a month off from rent when Dalton had a long streak of good luck. He won by a single point.

"I'm thinking I'm in the mood for spaghetti and meatballs," he said, with a languorous stretch. "With garlic bread. The real kind, not that stuff you buy at the grocery store."

"You're going to stink."

"That's right." He smiled. "Hopefully sooner, rather than later. I'm starving."

"I demand a rematch."

He shook his head. "This one was too close for

comfort. Think I'm gonna take a chance on losing out on all that home cooking? I'm no fool."

Bonnie heaved a long sigh. "I hope you're not," she said. "Suddenly it seems my future rides on it."

Chapter Three

"Every three minutes, guys think about sex. Take advantage of that."

—Dalton Price

"No."

"No?"

"No way."

Bonnie stopped in the lobby of the building in front of Dalton and Elissa. "No way what?" she asked Dalton.

"That outfit."

"What *now?*" Bonnie looked down at herself. "I bought this at Laura Ashley in London! It's one of my favorite dresses. It cost a *fortune.*"

Dalton and Elissa exchanged glances.

"Mrs. Malone has one like that," Elissa said, with a small frown. "But she's a lot older than you."

Dalton laughed and patted her shoulder. "Out of the mouths of babes."

"I'm not a baby, Dad."

"There she is!" An older woman with white hair and a shapeless flower-print dress shuffled out of the stairwell. Nelly Malone. "Ready to go, Lissy?"

Elissa nodded. Bonnie could tell she didn't like the nickname, but, thank goodness, she was too polite to say anything.

Nelly put her arm around the girl's shoulder and they began to walk toward the front door. "We'll see you two later."

"Have fun," Bonnie said, watching them go.

"Bye, Dad. Bye Bonnie," Elissa said.

"Bye, baby. Be smart in school today," Dalton told her with a proud smile.

"I'm sure she's *always* smart in school," Bonnie said and Elissa giggled. When the two had gone out the front door, Bonnie turned back to Dalton. "Mrs. Malone's dress was almost exactly like mine."

He laughed and gave a broad shrug. "Did you notice that, too?"

Bonnie looked at her watch. She had five minutes. Five minutes to change into something suitably alluring for her lunch with Mark today.

Dalton watched her, and said, as if reading her mind, "I'll give you a ride into the city. I have to go anyway."

"Are you sure?"

He nodded. "No problem. I go in a couple of times a week anyhow."

"All right. I'll be right back." She started to go, then stopped and turned back to him. "What should I wear?"

He looked blank. "Beats me. I'm no fashion expert. I just know what's bad when I see it."

"Do you know what's good when you see it?"

"Sure."

In for a penny, in for a pound. Bonnie decided to try this Dalton's way, at least this week. She hurried over to him, took his arm and pulled him toward the stairwell. "Then come with me."

He'd been in her apartment just two days ago, but he'd barely taken a glance at the place. He was in and out in a matter of half an hour, fixing the shower.

Dalton wasn't the type to snoop around.

Now, with Bonnie in it, the whole apartment came vibrantly to life, making him wonder how he'd managed to miss so much. He hadn't noticed the quirky little stone tabletop fountain in the foyer before. Or the cheap framed watercolors of Atlantic City on her bedroom walls. He knew the shop they'd come from. It had carried velvet black light posters in the early 1980s.

She stopped at the old-fashioned phone by the kitchen and called her friend Paula to tell her she wasn't going to be meeting her at the bus, then she led Dalton into her bedroom.

"Okay, wait here a sec," Bonnie told him, while she went into the walk-in closet. "I think I've got something you'll approve of."

He sat down on top of the embroidered spread on her bed, and thought immediately of being in it with her. He remembered what it felt like to have her in his arms. He remembered her kiss. It was a sweet thing. Something he'd had a hard time completely forgetting over the years. Not that he'd obsessed about it or anything, but Bonnie *had* lingered in his mind. Of course, that probably had more to do with the fact that they'd only been together the one time than because of any sort of woo-woo fate drawing them together.

So it made sense that he would help her find the man of her dreams. He cared about her, he wanted her to be happy, but it wasn't as if *he* could be the one to make her happy. As a matter of fact, given her description of the guy she was interested in, they were complete opposites. Which made it his duty, as a friend and an upstanding guy, to help her move on. Even though, at the moment, it sort of irritated him.

"What do you think?" She emerged from the closet in a deep red body-hugging sweater dress with a low V in the front. Every curve was hugged by the knit, and she looked like a bombshell.

"You look awesome," Dalton said, his mouth dry. He'd forgotten what an amazing body she had. How had he forgotten that? She must have been wearing those frumpy Nelly Malone clothes longer than he'd realized.

"Yeah?" She flushed.

He nodded. "A guy would have to be blind to overlook you in that."

She stepped in front of a full-length mirror and looked at her reflection skeptically. "I've never worn it before."

"So today's probably not the day to start. You don't want to look like you're trying too hard."

She looked relieved. "That's what I thought. Let me find something else."

"Make sure it doesn't make you look like Mrs. Malone," he cautioned. "You've got a lot of those outfits."

She poked her head out of the closet. "Cute, Dalton."

He shrugged. "Look, every three minutes a guy thinks about sex. So do you want him looking at you and thinking about sex with someone's grandmother, or do you want him to look at you and think about—"

"Got it," she called. "I want him to think about me. You don't have to go into graphic detail." A few minutes later she emerged again. "Okay, what about this?"

He looked up as Bonnie stepped out of the closet, wearing a tailored black skirt suit that revealed about a mile of leg and dipped tantalizingly low at the neck, showing a flash of skin. Skin he once knew the scent and taste of, skin he had run his hands over that hot summer night so long ago.

For just a moment, Dalton didn't breathe.

"I suppose this is more what you had in mind." She buttoned one of the buttons so the neckline wasn't quite so low, then looked at him. "Yes? Sort of sexy but still businesslike."

"Pretty good," he understated. "I say go with that one."

"That figures, because I'm *really* not comfortable in this." She buttoned another button, covering more skin.

"And you won't be until it makes you look like a nun," Dalton commented. "Next you'll be putting on long pants underneath it."

"The thought did occur to me."

"When did you become such a prude?"

"I've always been a prude, Dalton, you know that."

"Well, you're going to have to stop if you want to hijack this guy's attention."

She stopped buttoning and looked at him. "This might be a mistake."

"Exactly. Unbutton at least one." It wasn't that he had personal reasons for wanting her to do it. He just wanted to make sure she'd look as hot as he was sure she would. For her own sake, of course.

"Not that, *this*." She gestured between the two of them. "You and me doing this. Or, rather, *me* doing this." She walked over to the bed and plopped down on the side of it, next to him. "Maybe I don't want a guy I have to do this for."

Dalton watched her and nodded. "Maybe you don't want the guy you have to dress like an army man for either."

She gave a dry laugh. "Well, Mark Ford isn't a guy I have to dress like that for. He hated it."

Even though he'd never met him, Dalton wasn't feeling too lenient toward Mark Ford. "A guy should accept you for who you are."

She gave him a dry look. "So says the guy who's telling me to unbutton my shirt and hike up my skirt."

"Hey, we did *not* talk about the worthiness of the guy you wanted to attract. Our deal was not to help you *find* the man of your dreams, whoever that might be, it was to help you get one guy, the one who doesn't know you exist." He shook his head. "I never said it would be worth it."

She sighed and dropped her head into her hands. "But he would be worth it." She stood up, pulled her skirt slightly lower, and gave a firm nod. "He would be worth it."

"If you say so."

"You sound skeptical."

"Me? I'm always skeptical."

She eyed him for a moment, then said, "Okay."

"Let's go. You don't want to be late. We can talk about dinner in the car."

"Dinner?"

They started down the steps. "The dinner you're going to make for me tonight."

"Tonight?"

He didn't break his stride. "We made a deal."

"I know, but I figured you'd at least give me some notice."

"I am. Ten hours of it." He stopped at the front door and turned to look at her. "You got better plans tonight?"

She rolled her eyes. "No, but I hope to."

"I'm telling you, if he asks you out, you have to be unavailable." He opened the door and ushered her out, then followed. "And you have to make me spaghetti and meatballs."

She stopped again and looked back at him, impatience etched into her features. "Spaghetti and meatballs."

He shrugged. "My kid loves the stuff."

"I see. Well, in that case, I'll make it. For Elissa's sake." She walked toward his car and he smiled, watching the unintentional sway of her hips.

She was always at her best when she was completely unaware of her allure.

How could he teach her that?

By the time they were in the car, Dalton was starting to think maybe it wasn't right for him to be teaching Bonnie *anything* about winning over a man. Because men were pretty much jerks. Especially this guy if he'd somehow managed to miss or ignore Bonnie's attentions.

Dalton had been a jerk himself in his former life, he was willing to admit that, but now he could see that Bonnie was compromising herself in ways that clearly weren't comfortable for her. For a guy who couldn't possibly be worth that kind of sacrifice. Part of Dalton thought maybe he shouldn't be assisting her with that.

Then again, she was a grown woman. She could take care of herself. In fact, given the barbs she'd been throwing at him for the past twenty years or so, she'd always been more than able to take care of herself.

Plus, Dalton had never really known her to compromise her values. Not when it came down to it. Like in seventh grade when she refused—flat out *refused*—to dissect a frog in Mrs. Rhodes's science class, she'd told the teacher in front of God and everyone that she was willing to take a failing grade rather than give in and dissect.

And in the end, she'd gotten her way.

But she'd missed out on one of the coolest science projects they did in all of junior high.

Maybe all he had to do was help her win over this unworthy creep, so she could see for herself that it wasn't what she wanted.

"We've got fifteen minutes," Bonnie said, bringing him out of his thoughts. "There's no way you're going to get me to work on time."

"I'll get you there."

"I don't know about that." She clucked her tongue against her teeth. "Look at this traffic!"

"I've dealt with worse," he said, smoothly steering the old Toyota around a cab. He ignored the subsequent blaring horns and the alarmed look on Bonnie's face.

She checked the connection of her seat belt.

Dalton held back a laugh.

"Not funny, Dalton. If I wet my pants from fear, I don't think it's going to be too sexy."

"Not to the right kind of guy," he agreed, letting up on the gas.

"So," Bonnie said awhile later, her voice a little tight. "I have lunch with Mark today, and—"

"Mark?"

"The guy."

"Oh. Okay. Lunch with Mark. The guy. Got it." He glanced in her direction.

"Yes." She frowned at him. "You *are* still with me on this, aren't you?"

"Sure. I just forgot his name." He looked back at the road before him. "Go on. You have lunch with him today."

"Yes, to discuss painting his office."

"Sexy."

She sighed. "I know it's not ideal, but it's all I've got. So here's what I'm wondering. Should I ask him if he wants to go for drinks after work? You know, something slightly more intimate? Possibly suggestive of more, but also potentially casual." She clutched the arm rest as they swerved around a delivery truck then came to an abrupt stop at a red light.

Dalton looked at Bonnie. "You're going to lunch with the guy and you want to ask him out for drinks a few hours later?" The light in front of them turned green and Dalton steered around an older woman in a huge American car who remained stopped. "Nothing casual about that."

Bonnie groaned. "You're right. What do I do, then?"

"Wait for him to make the next move."

"That could take forever!"

"No way."

"No, I'm serious Dalton. He's been working with me for months and he hasn't made a single move so far."

Dalton gestured in her direction without taking his eyes off the road. "You haven't looked like this yet."

"And about that…are you sure I look okay?" She flipped the visor down, saw there was no mirror and put it up again, turning the rearview mirror instead.

"Hey, I need that."

"I'll give it back." She opened her purse and took out a lipstick, tracing it carefully over her mouth.

He watched for just a moment longer than he should have, and almost didn't notice the yellow school bus slowing to turn in front of him.

Granted they had a history. A history he remembered with ridiculous clarity, considering it had only been one night and it had happened about a hundred years ago. Still, after the initial few years of sheer hatred he'd felt for her in elementary school, Dalton had developed an attraction to Bonnie that had never entirely gone away. He'd hoped—in the naive way of a nineteen-year-old idiot kid—that sleeping with her would help him get over it, but instead it had increased his ardor. And that had scared him to death. He was leaving for school just a few weeks after that, and his scholarship was far too important—not only to him but to his entire family—for him to blow by obsessing over a girl back home.

Fortunately, she had spared him the trouble of rejecting her by rejecting him first. The only good thing was that *she'd* appeared to have forgotten about it.

"I feel like I look sort of…obvious," she said. "I don't want to look like I'm trying too hard."

"Then go easy on the lipstick."

"Yeah?" She took a tissue out of her purse and

dabbed her lips. "There," she said, turning the mirror back to exactly the right position, and smiling at Dalton with dewy-soft lips. "Better?"

He swallowed. "Just smile at him like that over lunch," he said to her. "He'll be putty in your hands."

"Smile at him? That's it? That's your expert advice?" She rolled her eyes. "I'm not sure I'm getting my money's worth."

"I didn't say this was going to be hard, Bon. All I said was that it would work."

"Do you think I didn't try smiling at him before?"

"From inside that circus tent of pink and yellow flowers you called a dress?"

She didn't answer, but instead turned her attention to the road before them. "It's the next block."

"I know where it is." He pulled the truck up in front of her building and stopped behind a delivery truck. "Okay, now, remember. Do *not* look eager. I don't care how good things are going, don't give yourself away. You can be friendly, smile, make eye contact, but do *not* ask him out for drinks. Got it?"

"All right." She collected her things.

"If you appear too eager he'll think you're easy. Maintain a little mystery."

"Gotcha." She started to open the door.

"And Bonnie?"

She stopped and turned back to him, still a little flushed. "What?"

"Button one of those buttons," he said, with half a smile. He just couldn't resist. "You're showing too much cleavage."

For lunch, Mark had chosen the loudest, cheapest restaurant on the block. It was one step up from a diner, and the lighting even made Mark look a little gaunt. She could only imagine what it was doing to her.

"Thanks so much for doing this," Mark said, handing her a menu. "I know you've got better things to do with your time."

"It's no problem," she said, smiling then wondering if the unflattering light gave her teeth the same greenish cast it gave the Formica table.

Mark's teeth, of course, were brilliant white.

They looked over their menus and ordered sandwiches. Then Bonnie opened her briefcase and took out some of the color swatches she'd chosen at the Home Center.

"The lighting here isn't the greatest," she understated, "but I thought this blue and this gray went together pretty well and would make the impact you were hoping for."

Mark took the swatches and examined them, tilting them at various angles, presumably to compensate for the fluorescent lighting. After half an hour of looking at other combinations, munching on a dry turkey club sandwich, and bestowing his charming smile on the waitress every time she refilled his coffee, he returned to the deep green and brown Bonnie had picked out initially.

"This is great." He smiled that even, movie star smile. "You've got excellent taste."

"Well, thanks."

He frowned and looked at her for a moment before saying, "I know maybe I shouldn't ask you this—"

She leaned forward slightly in her seat, thinking Dalton would approve the slight glimpse of skin this allowed the man in front of her. "Go ahead. What is it?"

Mark hesitated and Bonnie silently willed him to speak.

He did. "I hate to ask it since you've done so much already, but would you mind helping me find someone to do the work after hours?"

She moved back. "Oh. Well…"

"I shouldn't have asked," he said quickly. "After everything you've done here…"

Bonnie thought quickly. More help meant more time spent with Mark. And that was a good thing. Right? "I'm glad to do whatever I can to help," she said, with her most gracious smile. "Have you tried asking someone in building maintenance?"

"Not yet. Do you have a contact there?"

She thought about it for a moment. "Roger's the one who usually comes when there's a problem. He might be a good bet."

Mark gave That Smile again. "Man, I'd really appreciate your asking him."

"My—?" She was an executive. She'd worked her tail off in college, graduated cum laude, gotten a job at one of the most prestigious ad agencies in New York, and now this guy was asking her to act as his secretary?

She didn't like it.

They were interrupted by the waitress. "Anything else for you today?" she asked Mark.

He glanced at Bonnie. "Anything?"

"No, thanks."

"Just the check," he told the waitress, who took a pad out of her apron and scribbled on the top sheet before handing it to Mark.

Even upside down, Bonnie could see that the waitress had written her name—*Amber*—on the check and included her phone number. Please. Mark probably got that kind of thing all the time, but for a woman to do it when he was with another woman was just beyond tacky.

As was the fact that he ripped off that part of the check and put it into his pocket.

"So," he said, sliding the bill across the table toward Bonnie. "Should we just split it in half, or…?"

He didn't follow up on that *or.*

Or do you want to pay the whole thing?

Or should we just put a buck on the table and run for it?

Suddenly Bonnie was feeling distinctly uncharitable toward him. "Just tell me what I owe," she said.

He didn't appear to pick up on anything amiss in her tone. He lifted the bill and said, "It's nineteen seventy-six, so with a tip that's about, what, twenty-five bucks—"

He tipped generously.

That was a good sign. Proved he wasn't completely miserly.

Maybe he just didn't want to make Bonnie uncomfortable by paying the whole check like it was a date.

She took fifteen dollars out of her purse and put them down on the table, not wanting to look miserly herself.

He looked at it, then looked at her. "Listen, Bonnie." He leaned toward her slightly. "I feel really weird about this. How about you just let me pick up the check?"

As glad as she was to hear him say it, she wasn't sure how to respond. "Thanks, Mark. That's generous of you." She hoped it didn't sound sarcastic to say that to a guy like this about a place like this. Then again, he was the one who picked it.

He handed her money back to her. "I come from Iowa," he said, shaking his head "I'd never think twice about picking up the check there, but here in New York it's a whole different story. Powerful career women sometimes don't want a man to be a man. But you're not the heard-hearted type, I can tell that." He smiled, and Bonnie's soft heart skipped a beat or two. He really was so attractive. "Sometimes I guess I just have to follow my instincts. Sometimes we all do."

Really? Right now her instincts were telling her to run away, but her head kept reminding her how badly her instincts had failed her in the past. Mark was an excellent marital prospect. He had fantastic biological possibilities as a father. He made sense, on paper and in the flesh. So she had to keep with the plan.

Dalton's plan. She was giving it a single month to work.

If only Mark would ask her out so she could take the ridiculous step of saying no. That would be the true test of Dalton's plan.

Unfortunately, she didn't get the chance to test it out.

By the time she and Mark had walked back to the office and said their goodbyes to one another, Bonnie honestly couldn't figure out if things had gone well in the grand scheme of things or really badly. She mulled it over all afternoon and finally, on her way home, she took out her cell phone and called the one person she knew would be totally honest with her.

Chapter Four

"There's more than one way to a man's heart, but the stomach is a pretty reliable route."
                                                            —Dalton Price

"He wanted you to split the check?" Paula asked incredulously. "Dump him."

Bonnie put her cell phone earpiece in her ear and tucked the phone into her pocket as she walked up Broadway toward a small market she liked. "Number one, he's not mine to dump—"

"A technicality."

"—and number two, I told you he only suggested it *at first*. In the end, he not only paid it but he said he was just worried about offending me, the big scary city girl, by offering to pay. He actually said I wasn't hard-hearted like other women he'd met here."

"Oooh, he actually said you weren't hard-hearted?"

Bonnie stopped in front of the little mom-and-pop market she favored and opened the door for an elderly woman who was making her way out. "He meant it as a compliment. And I took it that way."

Paula wasn't buying it. "Know what? In my book, it's better to err on the side of offending someone by paying for them, than to err on the side of looking like a cheap bastard."

Bonnie couldn't help smiling at her outspoken friend. "Tell me what you really think."

"Sorry, but you don't come to me for sugarcoating."

"God knows." She picked up a shopping basket and went to the small produce department.

"And you're not going to get it from me when you want to go out with a deadbeat."

"Wait a minute, he's not a deadbeat. He paid." She dropped two onions in the basket and then rifled through the herbs looking for fresh basil.

Paula sighed, like she was talking to a somewhat dim-witted child. "It's not about who paid in the end—that is, it's not *only* about that—it's about intentions. And this guy intended for you to split the check. That's not chivalrous in my book."

Truthfully, it wasn't chivalrous in Bonnie's book either. But she'd had many occasions to question the relevance of that particular book since she'd been dating over the past decade. This wasn't the first occasion when she'd run into a guy who wanted to go dutch, and it wasn't the first time she'd wondered if it was unfair for her to expect otherwise. Was chivalry really a reasonable expectation these days? It wasn't the fifties anymore. People like Bonnie, who had grown up watching and loving Doris Day movies, were thrown by that. But there were plenty of people who had grown up without those old-fashioned ideas...was it right to penalize them for that?

"Paula, I don't think any of our books are doing us any good right now." Bonnie sighed, and moved from produce to the meat department. "How's the quest for the elusive, yet oh-so-attractive boss going?"

"Don't ask."

"I'm asking."

Paula groaned. "Let's just say he's not easy to get."

"Maybe he's married."

"I think I'd know if he was married."

"Would you know if he already had a girlfriend?"

"He doesn't. He's available. He's interested."

"How can you be so sure?"

"Bonnie." Paula let out a long sigh. "Okay, I don't want you to go ballistic or anything, but…he and I have already…you know…"

"Have already *what?*"

"You know…*been* together."

"You have not!"

Several people in the market turned and looked at her. But considering the fact that at least half of them were also on cell phones, Bonnie didn't feel too guilty. Such was the atmosphere in the city.

"Yes, we have. Well, almost. As close as you can get without, you know, going *all the way.*"

"When?" she asked in a whisper. "When did you have time? He's only been working there for a month. And why didn't you tell me this before?"

"Because I knew you'd react just like this."

"Just like *what?*" Bonnie heard her own tone bordering on harsh, and softened it. "I'm just disappointed that you didn't feel like you could trust me."

"It's not that I didn't trust you, Bon, it's just…I don't know. I guess I wasn't too proud of myself for doing it."

"Oh, honey—"

"No, no, it's okay. I've come to terms with it. Anyway, I think he's just freaking out about it now."

Bonnie took a number in front of the butcher's counter. "Does anyone else in the office know anything about his personal life?" Bonnie asked. "Can you get some scoop?"

"No one knows a thing. They don't even know about him and me. Truthfully, I'm tempted to go to one of those Internet sites where you can investigate someone."

"Ew."

"I know."

Her number was called and she stepped up to the counter. "Hang on, Paula. A pound and a half of meat loaf mix, please." The butcher nodded and Bonnie returned to her call. "Sorry."

"A pound and a half of meat loaf? You must be hungry."

"I'm cooking for Dalton tonight. Part of our deal."

"Cooking for Dalton." Now here was something Paula could latch on to, particularly since it didn't have anything to do with her private life. "What's for dessert?"

"Very funny." Dessert. She'd forgotten dessert. Elissa liked chocolate, so Bonnie decided to make a quick mousse.

"Honey, you are better off having metaphorical dessert in bed with Dalton Price than you are sharing sandwiches with cheapo Mark Ford. I don't care how hot he is, he can't be as hot as Dalton."

"And I don't care how hot you and the rest of the female population think Dalton Price is, he's still Dalton Price. There's no way I'd ever—" She remembered, all at once, that she was in a public place. "I've got to go, Paula. I'll call you later."

She hung up the phone, paid for her groceries and went back out into the balmy evening air.

She *didn't* care how hot Dalton was, she *wasn't* going to make the mistake of ever sleeping with him again. As for the mistake of believing there could be some kind of future with him?

She was *definitely* not going to make *that* mistake again.

Shortly after Bonnie got to Dalton's to make dinner, Elissa excused herself to watch a favorite TV show, leaving Bonnie with the uncomfortable sensation of making a romantic dinner for two rather than a cheap dinner for three.

"Do you want some wine?" Dalton asked, while Bonnie took the ingredients out of her shopping bags.

"Do you *have* wine?"

He gave her a look of exaggerated patience. "Yeah, a whole box of it." He went to the cabinet and took out a bottle of Australian merlot. "Sometimes I swear it's like you think we're still in second grade."

She looked at the bottle, then at Dalton. "I underestimate you, you mean. You're right. And I'm sorry."

"Don't worry about it," he said, taking a beer out of the fridge. He popped the top and raised the can toward her. "You're not all wrong about me."

She laughed. She had to. It was hard to resist a man who had a sense of humor about himself. "That's comforting."

He poured some wine in a glass and handed it to her. "But we're not kids anymore, Bon."

Something about the way he said it sent a thrill through her. "I know it. Sometimes it's hard to get used to that." She turned back to the counter to pull the basil leaves off the stems.

He walked up behind her and she could smell the light scent of beer on him. "Why are you still here?"

She turned to face him and was surprised to find him so close. "What do you mean? I'm making your dinner."

He smiled. "I mean here in Jersey. Here in Tappen. You could have moved on a long time ago. Why didn't you?"

"I did."

He raised an eyebrow. "Really?"

She nodded. "I went to school in Paris for a year, and got engaged to a guy I met there. We lived together in Seattle for almost two years."

"No kidding. I had no idea. What happened?"

"It didn't work out." She turned back to the counter. She didn't want to think about that brief moment in time when she'd been sure of where she was going and what her future held. Well, as sure as a person can be when it turns out they're completely and utterly wrong.

"Who was he?" Dalton persisted. "I never heard about this."

"What, you didn't get the memo?"

"When I left California I didn't leave a forwarding address."

"Wise move." She reached for a bowl and dropped the basil leaves in it.

He put his hand on her shoulder and turned her around to face him. "Come on. Tell me what happened." His blue eyes were warm, his face no longer that of the teenager she'd had a raging crush on but of a man. A man she saw every day. A man who could be her friend.

She sighed. "All right here's the short version. I

was twenty-two, he was twenty-three. His sister was eighteen, by the way. That's going to be relevant."

"This can't be good."

That was an understatement. "It's not. See, I had to travel some with my job back then and on one trip in particular I noticed Kirk was particularly hard to get in touch with. He was never home. Or never answering the phone. Whatever. When I came back he was different. More distant." This was embarrassing. "Two months later I found out why when his sister's good friend, who was also eighteen, turned out to be pregnant."

Dalton muttered an expletive.

"I left, needless to say. And they were married a couple months later." She turned back to the counter and put the meat in the bowl with the basil. "Maybe they still are, who knows? Got an egg?"

"Man, Bonnie, I'm sorry. I don't know what to say." He opened the refrigerator and handed her the egg.

She cracked it into the bowl. "There's nothing to say." Except that it was the last time in her life that she'd fully trusted someone. That she doubted her instincts about everything and everyone, man, woman and child alike now. And that she hated the weakness that fed that insecurity even while she knew, intellectually, that it came from her experience with *one* bad man.

It was also the reason she'd decided to pick a man with her head this time, and not her heart.

"Don't judge every man by that guy," Dalton said, as if reading her mind. "That kind of thing…" He shook his head in disgust. "That's the exception, not the rule."

"I know." She smiled and shook some salt and pepper over the meat. "That's where you come in, right?"

"Me?" He dipped his finger in the pot of bubbling spaghetti sauce she had on the back burner and tasted it.

"Keep your fingers out of the pot."

"I bet you say that to all the guys."

"I do if I don't know where their fingers have been." She looked at him narrowly. "Or if I do."

"Ooh. Harsh."

She shook her head. "Seriously now. You're going to help me win over Mark Ford, right?"

"Oh. Yeah. Right."

"So. To that end—" she was eager to change the subject from her failed romance "—what do I do next?"

"I think you mix all that stuff together," he said, nodding at the bowl. "And that spaghetti sauce? Awesome."

She gave him a look. "Thanks, but I mean with Mark. What do I do next with Mark?" She put her hands in the bowl and started mixing the meat with the seasonings.

"You should find a way to cook for him."

"Cook? Are you speaking literally or metaphorically?"

He laughed. "Interesting question. But I meant literally. There's a reason they say the way to a man's heart is through his stomach."

"I've worked really hard to be taken seriously in the business world," Bonnie told him, starting to roll the meatballs. "I don't want to blow that now by walking into the office in an apron carrying a platter of homemade cookies."

"You never know, that might play right into one of his fantasies."

Bonnie gave him an exasperated look.

"Okay, okay, leave the apron at home. But cookies are a good idea. Or you could just take an extra large portion of that lasagna your mom used to make for all the church potlucks, and offer half of it to him."

She was touched. "You remember my mom's lasagna?"

"Oh, my God, who doesn't? One bite and you're hooked. I would have married your mom myself."

Bonnie couldn't help but laugh. "Who knew it was so easy to get to you?"

"Now you know my little secret." He shrugged. "Food is a sensual thing. Taste, smell, touch." He glanced at her hands, then back into her eyes. "It's very sensual."

Bonnie rolled her eyes but something about the way he was talking disquieted her deep inside. She dropped the meatballs into a pan on the stove and tried to make light of the situation so Dalton wouldn't figure out that he was giving her unholy thoughts. "I do have to say, this is very similar to Leticia Bancroft's advice. And she was way cheaper than you."

He shrugged. "It's the difference between an exercise video and a personal trainer. I'm giving you the facts as you go along. Plus I'm not going to tell you to wear an army uniform."

She opened her mouth to object but decided not to bother. The green clothing had been an unmitigated disaster.

"So now," he went on. "You need to find a way to work some aphrodisiacs into your repertoire."

"Right. 'Hey Mark, I just happened to bring some extra oysters Rockefeller and champagne, do you want some?' I think he'd see through that."

"It's good advice, Bon. Take it or leave it."

She sighed. "All right. But if I get a reputation as

a Betty Crocker wannabe, you are going to hang for it, buddy." She turned the meatballs on the skillet.

"Betty Crocker was hot. You're a gorgeous woman, add a little something extra and you've got him."

"Fine." She nodded, replaying, three times in rapid succession, the sound of Dalton Price calling her a "gorgeous woman." "And thanks. I'm not so sure about this, but I'll give it a try."

"Good. And wear something sexy."

"Sexy? Just what do you have in mind, Dalton? A thong? Maybe a G-string?"

The way he looked her over made her feel, for a moment, as if she weren't wearing anything at all.

"You got those things?" he asked her.

"No." She still felt the residual thrill of his look fizzling in her blood.

He shrugged. "That's too bad." He sucked breath in through his teeth. "You looked excellent in them."

"What are you talking about? How could I look excellent in them when you've never seen me in them because *I don't have them?*"

"It's all in here." He tapped his temple with his index finger and, at her outraged expression, he laughed. "Man, you are such a sucker."

"You've said that." Her face felt warm, though it wasn't entirely without pleasure.

He smiled and looked at the stove. "How's that dinner coming along?"

She looked at the meatballs smoking in the skillet and gave a quick exclamation. "Get out of here, Dalton. You're distracting me."

He chuckled and touched his finger to her cheek, making her skin tingle with warmth. "I'll take that as a compliment."

"You would," she said, with a smile. She didn't add the uncomfortable truth beneath her words: that he could.

Chapter Five

"Make him think you're not interested. There's nothing a man finds more attractive than a woman who doesn't want him."

—Dalton Price

The dinner Bonnie made was excellent, just as Dalton knew it would be. But he hadn't counted on how much Elissa would enjoy her company. That had been a surprise.

"This is *so good*," Elissa gushed, taking a third helping of spaghetti. Her face and clothes were dotted with sauce. "Can you teach me to cook, Bonnie?"

"Sure," Bonnie said with a warm smile. When she looked at the child, she gave her her full attention. "I'd love to."

"Maybe you can teach Daddy, too," Elissa said. "He's terrible."

"Hey. I'm not a terrible cook. No one can heat up a frozen dinner better than I can."

"But you always leave ice chunks in the middle!" Elissa giggled.

"Ugh," Bonnie said.

"Okay," Dalton conceded. "So some people could do a better job at heating them than I can. But can they fix an air conditioner?"

Bonnie shook her head. "I can't. And you did a great job on the shower, I have to admit. The water pressure hasn't been that good since I moved in here."

"There." He gestured at her with the most excellent garlic bread he'd ever tried. "See? It all evens out."

"Unless we starve to death," Elissa said, and Bonnie burst out laughing.

"She's got you there," Bonnie said, and her blue eyes were bright with laughter.

He'd always been a sucker for her eyes.

"I don't like this ganging up business," Dalton said, but in truth he did. It was great to see Elissa bonding with Bonnie. It had been a year since her mother—a struggling actress in L.A. who didn't want a "family image" to diminish her marketability as a bimbo bit player—had bothered to visit with her, and as a general rule he tried to keep his dates separate from his home life unless the relationships seemed to have some promise of longevity.

So far none had.

So it made sense that Elissa should bond with a friend of his, rather than a girlfriend. Much less danger of a dramatic and/or abrupt exit from the relationship.

An hour passed in almost no time at all, and when they were finished eating dinner, Elissa went back to her room to finish homework and Bonnie washed the dishes while Dalton dried.

"So I've been thinking about advertising this place," Bonnie said, scrubbing the skillet. "And what I came up with is a coupon."

"What do you mean a coupon?"

"Well, what I was thinking was something like sign a two-year lease, get one month's rent free."

"*Free?* That's crazy."

"No crazier than ignoring a guy you're trying to seduce."

"No, *that* makes sense. In that case, you're making the goods more attractive."

"Same theory here. Free rent makes a place look attractive."

"Sure, but at a considerable expense."

"Look, if you secure a two-year lease, isn't it worth it? Rather than having an empty apartment?"

He thought about it. "Maybe. But maybe not. I'd rather just lease the units straight before resorting to desperate measures."

Bonnie scoffed. "Oh, come on, that's not a desperate measure. You can take the loss on your taxes *and* net more money." She rinsed the skillet and handed it to him. "It's win-win for you."

"I'll have to do the math."

"I already did it. It's in the other room, I'll give it to you when we finish here." She rinsed her wineglass and put it in the dishwasher. The party was over. "Trust me, this is the best move you can make. You'll earn far more than you lose." She pulled the dishwasher door shut and wiped her hands on the front of her jeans. "Finished."

"That was a great dinner, Bon. Really. Thanks."

"No problem." She walked into the living room and picked up a folder from the end table by the sofa. "Here's a workup of my idea." She handed it to him.

He opened the folder. She had made a sample

ad and coupon, with a small sketch of the building that he recognized from the old stationery in the rental office. There was also a detailed spreadsheet with profits and loss outlined. "Wow. That's a lot of work."

She waved the notion away. "It's what I do all the time. It's not a big deal."

But he knew it was. She had to have spent a considerable amount of time on it.

"If you like it," she said, "I can get it camera ready for you. Then you can just give it to the newspaper to run."

"Thanks." He looked at her. "Really. This is amazing."

"Remember you said that."

"I will." He put the folder down and walked Bonnie to the door. "So tomorrow you're taking some food in to work with you, right? Something you made yourself?"

"Right." She pulled the door open and turned to face him. "I think it's insanely ill-guided but I'll try it."

"Good. Let me know how it goes."

"Oh, I will."

He laughed at her skeptical tone. "Trust me."

"I'm trying." She raised her eyebrows, then smiled before she left. "But it ain't easy."

* * *

Bringing food to work as a ploy to win over a man?

Bad plan. Stupid plan. She'd put the Tupperware container in the fridge in the morning and by noon the thing had been ransacked. Four hours of constructing lasagna the night before had been wasted on some jerk who had seen it in the fridge and felt free to just dig in. Whoever it was didn't even appear to have heated it up first, they just ate it cold.

After spending half the night making the stupid lasagna, Bonnie was pretty ticked when she found it decimated that way. It wasn't as if she could offer Mark even one tidy portion of it. Whoever had dug in had literally dug in.

"What's the matter?" Lena Zuranski, one of Bonnie's co-workers, asked when she came into the kitchen. "You look like someone just punched you in the gut."

"It's—" Bonnie put the lid back on the Tupperware. "Nothing."

"Oh, was that *yours?*" Lena asked.

Bonnie frowned. "Y-yes. Did you—you didn't eat this, did you?"

Lena acted embarrassed, although she didn't particularly *look* embarrassed. "Deb told me she had some pasta in the fridge and I opened that up and gobbled it right down. I had no idea it wasn't Deb's until just now when she told me hers was in a blue container." She shrugged. "I'm sorry. I've just found out I'm pregnant and I'm eating everything in sight."

"It's okay." Bonnie held the container out to her. "Want the rest?"

"I couldn't, thanks." She waved it off. "I'm stuffed." It wasn't unlike borrowing a handkerchief and giving it back used.

Bonnie looked at it with some distaste. "Okay."

Lena gave a little wave and smile and left the room. When she was gone, Bonnie looked once more into the container and then shrugged and put it back in the fridge.

She'd eat later.

As it turned out, she didn't see Mark for the rest of the day anyhow, so the jury was out on whether or not the lasagna was worth making. Sure, if it had been perfect—as it had been when she brought it in—she might have sought him out, but she'd never know now. Instead she sat in her office and drank diet cola and wondered if *any* of the advice she was getting was worth a damn.

By the end of the day, she'd decided it wasn't and she left work in a foul mood, which hadn't been alleviated by the time she saw Dalton outside their building.

"Did you make the lasagna?"

"Yes," she hissed. "I did. In fact, I was up until 1:00 a.m. making the stupid lasagna."

"Aw, man, are there any leftovers?"

She gestured toward the door. "Only about twelve pounds of it. Come on up."

He took her up on it, following her to her apartment and sitting on a bar stool while she cut a couple of slices of lasagna from the fridge and put them on a plate in the microwave.

"The lasagna didn't work on Mike?"

"Mark. No, but in fairness, it's quite possibly because a pregnant woman tucked into it with what appeared to be her bare hands before I ever got the chance to offer it to Mark."

"Ouch." Dalton looked at the microwave. "Is that almost done?"

She followed his gaze. "There's another minute and a half. Like it says on the display."

"I was hoping you'd overestimated."

She rolled her eyes and took out two plates. "Hungry, huh?"

"Starving."

"Me too."

They watched the display count down to zero, then she took the platter out, pushed one of the slices onto a plate for Dalton and handed it to him. "Consider this meal number two."

"No fair!"

"No?" She reached for the plate. "You don't want it."

"You fight dirty, Miss Vaness."

She raised an eyebrow. "Does that mean you're giving it back or agreeing to knock another meal off my tally."

"I'm keeping it," he grumbled. "As long as I get seconds."

"Fine."

"And thirds."

"I can put the whole thing in a nose bag for you if you want."

"No, thanks. The plate should do just fine." He balanced a generous bite onto his fork and shoved it into his mouth. "Mmm." He nodded approvingly and gave her the thumbs-up. "This woulda worked," he added, his mouth full.

She rolled her eyes. "Thanks. And learn some manners, would you?"

"Sure," he said, his mouth full again. "Anything you say."

"So what's my next move with Mark, coach?" she

asked. "Aren't you supposed to be concentrating on my game plan rather than my lasagna?"

"I have room for both," he said, cutting another piece with the side of his fork. "Next we return to plan A."

"Which was...?"

"Ignore him."

"Ignore him," she repeated.

Dalton nodded. "It's simple human nature. People want what they can't have. At this point you've been totally available to him—"

"I have not!"

"Yes, you have. He says 'jump' and you say 'how high and where should I land?'"

Bonnie rolled her eyes but she knew Dalton was more right than wrong.

"So now," he went on. "You just need to be a little hard to get for awhile."

"With all due respect, Dalton, I have tried this sort of thing in the past and it hasn't worked." She was thinking of him. After their one night together, she'd been too shy to pursue him so she'd instead stayed away from any place he might have gone so she didn't have to face him. She had, essentially, removed herself completely from his realm. And it had *not* made him call.

He frowned slightly and for one terrifying moment she actually thought maybe he'd been able to read her mind. "You didn't try it before. I *told* you to try it but you ignored me."

She batted her eyelashes at him. "Did it make you find me irresistible?"

He smiled and shoved another mountain of lasagna into his mouth, and said, "I'm here, aren't I?"

"You're a charmer."

"I know it." He took a swig of the water she'd put on the counter for him. "Now listen, I'm serious. Try being completely unavailable to this guy. It works on most of us."

She sighed. There was no way she could argue this further without ending up admitting something she did *not* want to admit. "All right. But what if he doesn't notice my unavailability?"

"So you make him notice it." He said it like it was the most obvious thing in the world. "Make him notice *you*. You're a beautiful woman, but even you can't just hide without taking the chance of being forgotten. Guys think about what's in front of them. Out of sight, out of mind, you know. You have to be right in front of him, almost within reach, but—" he splayed his hands "—unavailable."

"Right in front of him," she said, moving in front of Dalton to refill his glass.

He watched her. "Exactly. So close that he could almost touch you. But he can't."

Surprised by his tone, Bonnie looked at him, just in time to see his blue gaze rake up her figure. "Maybe he doesn't want to," she said.

"He'd have to be crazy."

She faced him, hand on her hip. "That's nice of you to say, but, sadly, not every man in the world is crazy if he doesn't want me. Take yourself, for example."

"Me?"

"Just for an example. Not with me, of course, but with anyone. There must be plenty of women out there who aren't interested in you." She grinned. "Why don't you have a girlfriend?"

"This isn't about me."

"So you're not attracted to anyone?"

He raised his eyebrows. "Who says?"

"Are you saying you are?"

"This isn't about me." He smiled.

"Oh, no, no, no, you're not getting away with that so easily. Do you have a secret girl out there somewhere?"

"Yeah, she's downstairs watching TV."

"Elissa." Bonnie smiled. "She'll leave you for another man someday, you know."

"Don't they all?"

Bonnie's eyebrows shot up. "*Do* they?"

"Nah."

Of course they didn't. "You don't like talking about yourself much, do you?"

"This isn't about me," he said, yet again.

Maybe it wasn't but part of Bonnie couldn't resist the urge to dig into his psyche and try and figure out what made Dalton tick. Or not tick, as the case may be.

"So what kind of girl do you like?" Bonnie asked, pulling some melted cheese off the top of the lasagna and popping it into her mouth. "What's your type?" She pulled up a bar stool and sat next to him in front of the counter.

He leaned back and surveyed her. "For one thing, I like a girl who doesn't talk with her mouth full."

She nodded vigorously, chewing. "I understand that. With you there. What else?"

He laughed. "A good sense of humor."

"Amen!"

"Intelligence." He held up a finger. "Wait, I should have said that first. That's a must. I can't spend ten minutes with a stupid girl, no matter what she looks like."

"I'll bet," Bonnie scoffed, thinking of a photo of

his ex-wife Elissa had shown her in a tabloid magazine. The woman was gorgeous. A real bombshell.

"I'm serious," Dalton said. "And while you're at it, add character to the list. Good values. Old-fashioned, you might say."

Bonnie frowned. "Where does your ex fit into this picture? Or does she?"

He gave a humorless spike of a laugh. "When do you think I got my priorities straight? I've had plenty of time to hone this list since I left California."

She nodded, more serious. "So what's the problem? Just can't find the right person?"

"Who said there's a problem?" He shook his head and raked his fingers across his hair in that way he used to when a teacher called on him and he didn't know the answer. "You're making a lot of assumptions."

"Because every time I ask if there *is* someone, you dodge the question."

"Why do you want to know?"

"Because you know *everything* about my love life, and I know *nothing* about yours."

"Good."

"I don't like it that way. It's not fair." She was ribbing him, but she could tell he knew she was partly serious.

"Since when is life fair?"

"Come *on,* Dalton."

"Okay." He looked at her steadily. "Yes, there's someone. Satisfied?"

Bonnie swallowed. Suddenly she wasn't having as much fun as she had been. She'd been pretty sure he'd say no and she could continue her semi-flirtatious game. "Anyone I know?"

Still keeping his gaze even upon her, he shook his head. "No. Not at all."

"Oh." What had she been hoping? That he'd say *yes, it's you* and sweep her into his arms? "So I guess I can't warn her about you." She added a lame *ha ha* to the end of that but it still sounded a little harsh. "I'm kidding, of course."

He smiled. "She wouldn't listen to you anyway."

"Oh. Well." She shrugged. "There you go." She stood up and started to put the plates in the sink. "Do you want to take any of this home with you?"

"Yes. Please. Whatever you don't want." He stretched and put a hand on his belly, Buddha-style. "You're an awesome cook."

"Thanks." She reached under the counter and took out a plastic container. "I wish Mark thought so."

"He will," Dalton said.

She scooped the heavy noodles and sauce into the

container, then wiped the edge with a clean cloth before putting the lid on, just as her mother—famous for making 'to go' packages for friends, had always taught her. "Here you go." She handed it to him. "Don't eat it all in one sitting."

He chuckled and started for the door. "Elissa's in on this too. Even I can't eat this much." He glanced down at the food. "Not right now anyway." He stopped at the door and turned back to her. "So you're going to play hard-to-get, right?"

It took her a moment to realize what he meant. "Tomorrow? Yes. I'll try it. But I think it's stupid."

"Not as stupid as being right there waiting for him all the time." He gave her a quick wink. "Trust me."

Her breath caught in her throat. *Trust me.* He'd said that to her before. And even though she knew this time circumstances were different and she could, indeed, trust him, something inside of her was disquieted. "I'll give it a try," she said. "But I'm not making any guarantees."

He looked at her for a long moment before turning to start down the hall. "There are no guarantees in life. But I'll give you as close to one as I can. If this guy doesn't take some serious notice of you soon, there's got to be something wrong with him."

Bonnie watched Dalton saunter down the hall

without looking back, and she wondered if he really believed what he was saying, or if this was all just a game to him.

Chapter Six

"Jealousy is a powerful motivator for men."
—Dalton Price

Dalton was wrong. Wrong wrong wrong. He
couldn't have been *more* wrong if he'd tried.

In fact, Bonnie was beginning to wonder if he *was*
trying because some of his advice was so patently crazy.

First of all, she'd had to go out of her way in the
office corridors to *look* for Mark in order to then ignore him. Several times this resulted in her finding
herself inadvertently close to the men's room door,

or the office of a painfully talkative Isaac Asimov fan who had stopped to chat with Bonnie on his way to the restroom with a large volume tucked under his arm.

In an office with sixty-four other employees, she needed better advice than to ignore one. She needed to figure out how to call attention to herself in a positive way. So far, she was pretty sure she'd given Mark the idea that she was a little off balance.

Not the impression she was going for.

"How'd it go?" Dalton asked when she got to his door that evening. He must have seen the answer in her face before she spoke because he quickly added, "That well, huh?"

"Oh, yeah, the ignoring game was a *rousing* success." She didn't wait to be invited, but walked in and plopped down on his sofa. "He was masterful at it."

"*He* was masterful at it?"

"Oh, yes. I barely got a chance to ignore him because he was so busy not noticing me."

Dalton sat down on the sofa facing her. "Slow down. What are you talking about?"

Bonnie took a breath. "You, Leticia Bancroft, the Rules, *everyone* is wrong. These games aren't getting me anywhere. Today I went in to work, oozing fake confidence, I was absolutely charming to everyone, especially if Mark was within earshot. But every time I felt like I might have his attention, however briefly, I'd look at him and he'd just look away." She narrowed her eyes at Dalton. "He didn't say a single word to me."

Dalton looked at her for a few moments, with an expression she couldn't quite read but assumed—incorrectly—was shame. Then he laughed. "That's perfect."

"Perfect?"

"Yeah. Can't you see? It means it worked. He was *watching* you. He was stupefied by your charm. Rendered voiceless."

"Stupefied by my charm? Rendered voiceless?" Bonnie raised an eyebrow. "You could put a spin on anything. Ever think about going into politics?"

"Bonnie, Bonnie, Bonnie." He clicked his tongue against his teeth, shook his head in a patronizing manner and put his hand on her shoulder. "I'm telling you, the fact that you caught him looking at you is a good thing. How could it not be?"

"It could not be because he *didn't say a word to me.* He wasn't moved to ask me out or compliment my stupid low-cut outfit or ask if I liked dogs or *anything.* He looked at me from the corner of his eye now and then and went about his business. That's not interest, Dalton, that's…" She gestured, searching for a word: "BLAH. It's nothing."

He took his hand off her shoulder and shook his head. "That's not true." It was immature, of course, but he knew it wouldn't do a lot of good for him to point out the guy's worst qualities for Bonnie right now. She never said she wanted Dalton to help her win over a great guy, she said she wanted *that* guy.

No matter how stupid, blind and worthless he was.

Even Dalton was better for her than that, he told himself. Did this guy appreciate all the great things about her? Did his heart skip a beat when she walked into a room? Did he find himself fumbling over his words, even though they saw each other every day? Dalton doubted it.

"It's not true? You're trying to say this is good?"

"It's great. Just what you want."

Bonnie stared at him for a moment. "Are you serious or are you just trying to shut me up?"

"I'm totally serious."

She clearly wasn't convinced. "All right, say you're serious and you're right—and I'm not saying you're either because frankly I think you're neither."

"Okay," he prompted, holding back a smile.

"This experiment is now done. It didn't work."

"You don't know that!"

"I do. Every instinct I have tells me Mark isn't responding to me at all."

Dalton thought about that for a moment. "Look, I don't want to point out the obvious here, but are you sure this guy's not gay?"

She hesitated, looking, for a moment, like a deer in the headlights. "Yes, I'm sure," she answered firmly, but there was *no, I'm not sure* written in her eyes.

"You're sure you're sure?"

She nodded impatiently. "Yes! Don't try and weasel out of responsibility for your bad advice by implying he's gay."

"I'm not, everything's going fine. You just don't realize it yet."

She raised an eyebrow. "So my plan is working like a charm?"

He gave a half shrug. "I'm not sure about a *charm* but, yeah, it's working just fine."

"In that case, what do I do next? If I pay warm fuzzy attention to him now he'll think I'm schizophrenic."

"So now you do more of the same," Dalton said simply.

She sighed and looked at him through narrowed eyes. "More ignoring him?"

"Exactly."

He *looked* serious. And sane. Nevertheless, she

thought it was a terrible suggestion. "Dalton Price, you're crazy. If I'd paid you for this advice, I would demand my money back."

He rolled his eyes. "Okay, okay, you can take a slightly more aggressive approach if you want."

"So I don't ignore him?"

"No, you do. But you *also* make him jealous." He held his hands up to stop the objection he knew was coming. "I was going to save this for later, but if you're that eager, you can try it now. It's a desperate measure, but I think it will make you feel better."

"Oh, boy." She sighed. "So far it's making me feel nervous. How am I going to make him jealous if he doesn't even notice me when I'm right in front of him?"

"He'll notice this."

"*This* being…?"

"Pay a little bit of attention to another guy in front of him. Nothing overt. I'm not telling you to jump some guy's bones in the copy room, but just, you know, play it up a little. That ought to drive Mike crazy."

"Mark."

"Sorry?"

"His name is Mark." She frowned. "You have a terrible memory for names, you know that? Anyway, how can I flirt with some other guy in the office without making him, whoever he is, think I'm interested in *him?* Believe me, there's no one else there I want to give that impression to."

Dalton thought about it. "Do you run into this Mark guy anywhere else? A health club or regular lunch joint or something like that?"

She thought of the greasy diner where they'd had lunch. "We don't really have the same taste. I know where he lives, but I can't exactly go hang out on street corners flirting with strangers."

"No," Dalton agreed. "I definitely don't recommend that. Wrong impression entirely." He thought about it again for a moment, then said triumphantly, "I've got it."

"What?"

He looked quite pleased with himself. "There's one place you can find him at the same time every day."

"Yeah, in the office."

"And in the office building. Where there are other people who don't work for your company."

That was true. Everyone passed through the bustling lobby every morning before work. And she'd noticed that Mark was very punctual; a quality she appreciated about him. He came in every single day at 8:45 a.m. Which meant five minutes before that, he'd be in one predictable spot. "By the elevators."

Dalton smiled and pointed at her. "Bingo."

This was good. This could work. *This* made sense. "Can you do it tomorrow?"

"Me?" Dalton looked surprised. "Why me? Isn't there a security guard or someone like that you can use? All you need to do is pay attention to another man while Mike is passing by. It's not exactly a three-act play."

She thought of sixty-something bald Murray, who had worked security in the building for as long as she'd worked there, and who she had never seen out from behind the entry desk. She couldn't even swear he had legs. "Not if I want to capture Mark's attention in a *positive* way," she said dryly. "Come on, Dalton. It's your idea. You'll know how to play it perfectly. In one act," she added. "Please?"

He considered her for a couple of uncomfortably long seconds before saying, "Filet mignon."

"When?"

"Tomorrow."

She pretended to have to think about it, but they both knew she didn't have any other plans for after work. "Fine. Meal number three. This'll be over before you know it."

He clicked his tongue against his teeth. "Come on, Bon, the way you talk I almost get the feeling you don't *like* cooking for me."

"Yeah, well, I'm getting the impression that you're liking it a little too much. I'm terrified you're going to find some loophole that'll lock me into this deal forever."

He gave a rakish grin. "That's not a loophole, that's marriage. Close, but not exactly the same thing."

She laughed. "You're not tricking me into either."

"You're a hard woman, Bonnie Vaness." He drew a breath in through his teeth. "I like that."

He was completely joking, but Bonnie still felt her heart give a little trip.

"Let's just stick to the plan, Dalton. The plan for me to seduce Mark Ford."

He blew air into his cheeks and then out. "All right. So you're going to have to make him jealous."

"And not with the guy in accounting who leaves for the bathroom every day at noon with a huge science fiction book under his arm."

"I'll do it," Dalton decided. "I'll drive you into the city tomorrow and bait this guy with you."

"You will? Really?"

"Yes." He held up a cautionary finger. "But if I get a parking ticket, it's on your head."

She held out her hand, for the first time confident that she was on the right track. "Deal."

Chapter Seven

"Step back every once in a while and ask yourself if the guy is really worth it."

—Dalton Price

"You gotta touch me."

"What are you talking about?" Bonnie whispered.

They were standing in the marble lobby of the Parkington Building in lower Manhattan, where Bonnie worked on the twenty-fourth floor. People were bustling around them, as Bonnie and Dalton stood facing each other, trying to create some sort of show that might get Mark Ford's notice.

Bonnie could hear her grandmother's disapproval ringing in her mind's ear, *It's not seemly to touch in public. Some things should be saved for the privacy of home, and sometimes they're not even appropriate there.*

"What if someone we know comes through here?" she whispered to Dalton.

"It's what you're counting on, isn't it?"

Her face went warm. "I mean someone other than—" She spotted Mark entering the revolving door. "Oh! There he is. He's coming in the building now."

"So touch me. Quick."

"Where?"

"Anywhere," Dalton whispered harshly. "Brush something off my shoulder. Or my cheek. Or unzip my pants."

She gave him an exasperated look.

"And, I can't overstate this, look like you like me. *Smile,*" he added, when she didn't.

She smiled broadly and lightly brushed his shoulder awkwardly, saying through her teeth, "Can you see him?"

Dalton caught her wrist and pulled her in close, for what could have been a long-time-no-see hug, or something far more intimate. Bonnie's thoughts leaped to the more intimate. He smelled great. Soap and skin. None of the expensive, perfumy cologne so many of her co-workers favored. She wondered if Mark smelled as sexy up close.

"I don't know who he is," Dalton whispered, then drew back and laughed loudly.

She glanced surreptitiously toward the door. "Over there at the entrance. Blond hair. Blue eyes."

"Him?" The surprise in Dalton's voice sounded genuine. "That guy? Are you serious?"

"Yes. What do you mean *that guy?* Have you got some sort of problem with him?"

Dalton's face was etched with distaste. "I just can't believe he's your type."

"He's not. That's what I like about him. Now stop judging and start helping me." She glanced back at Mark. "Darn it, he's stopped. He's dialing his cell phone." Bonnie watched as Mark put the phone to his ear, then she said, "Quick, hug me again, I don't think he saw it the first time." She threw herself against Dalton and pulled close, as if he was a pal she hadn't seen in fifteen years.

It felt great. He was so manly, so powerful and strong. Dalton was the perfect specimen to make Mark jealous and she was sure this would work. How could Mark look at Dalton and not assess his own manliness? It would be like Bonnie standing next to

Cindy Crawford without wondering if her own hair and makeup looked okay.

"We don't need to actually share a spleen in order to make him jealous," Dalton whispered, pulling back slightly. His face was a little flushed.

Had she hugged him that tightly?

"Now, make sure you say hello as he passes," he said, maintaining the slight distance he had just put between them.

"Then what?"

"Then we'll improvise." He gazed into her eyes, and even though it was for the benefit of onlookers—well, one onlooker in particular—Bonnie's heart did a funny little trip.

He was *masterful,* she thought cynically. Dalton Price had a raw animal magnetism that appealed to women on the most basic level. He had to, if even Bonnie was susceptible to it.

He reached out and took her hands in his. Tingles shot up both her arms.

"How about we went to school together," he said. "We're seeing each other for the first time in years. I'm enamored of your beauty and yada yada yada." He touched her hair and shook his head, outwardly musing, "Bonnie Vaness. I can't believe it's you."

"Mark!" She said, a little too loud, as she spotted

Mark passing them by. Tingles showered down her spine from Dalton's touch.

Mark stopped, looking a little startled, then smiled when he saw Bonnie. "Hey Bonnie." He glanced uneasily at Dalton, then back to her. "You're in late today, aren't you? You're always at your desk before me."

"That's my fault," Dalton said, giving that movie-star smile he usually reserved for weak females. "I've just run into her and I can't let her get away that fast."

Good, Bonnie thought, watching him. Dalton made an extremely handsome would-be suitor. A guy would have to be nuts, or really confident, or maybe both, in order not to take notice.

Dalton held his hand out to Mark. She watched, noticing how much stronger Dalton's hands looked than Mark's pale, long-fingered ones. And did Mark get manicures? She hadn't noticed that before. "Dalton Price. I went to school with Bonnie years ago and—" he looked at her with convincing adoration "—have just had the excellent fortune to run into her this morning."

Bonnie was amazed at his acting skills. He looked as if he were totally smitten. "Dalton works for—"

"Bennett Milton, if I'm not mistaken," Mark interrupted her, looking at Dalton with interest. "Out on the West Coast?"

Dalton looked surprised. "That's right. Well, it *was*." He frowned, as if trying to place Mark. Never one to give away too much information about himself, he asked, "Have we met?"

Mark shook his head. "No, but I worked for Fennifield Advertising in San Diego a few years ago. One of my colleagues worked with your company on an ad campaign after all the dot-coms went under."

Dalton's eyes lit with remembrance. "Yes, Erin Wakeman."

"That's right." Mark nodded.

Bonnie's stomach tightened.

"Boy, she was something else," Dalton went on.

"You're telling me." Mark gave a nudge-nudge-wink-wink laugh. "She must have mentioned your name a hundred times. Said you were a real crackerjack investor. I'd love to set up a consultation with you sometime, if you're available."

Bonnie nudged Dalton with her foot. She did *not* want him taking over Mark's attentions.

He got the hint. "I'm really just here for the day. So how do you know Bonnie?" he asked Mark, giving her another of those pseudo-admiring looks that was so credible she almost believed it herself.

"We work together," Mark said, moving fractionally closer to her in what could have been interpreted as a semi-possessive movement.

Dalton must have picked up on that because he also moved just slightly closer. It was clearly a possessive move, or meant to look like one. "Lucky you," he said, with a rueful shake of the head. "I'd love to look at this face every morning."

Bonnie's face felt warm. "Thanks, Dalton."

Mark looked at her and nodded, "She's just great."

A few weeks ago, this would have encouraged her but this morning she felt...nothing. It was probably because of the crowd and the nerve-racking stress of putting on this act.

"Well, hey, it was good meeting you Mark," Dalton said to him, then turned to Bonnie. "Look, can I give you a call sometime? I'd love to take you to dinner."

Bonnie blanched. What should she do? Refuse and take a chance on looking snotty? Or agree and look interested in another man in front of Mark?

Fortunately, Mark saved her from having to answer. "That reminds me, Bonnie, I was hoping you might let me take you to dinner tonight."

She raised her eyebrows and glanced at Dalton, who was frowning. Was he doubting her ability to play it cool? Well, now was her chance to show him he could. "Thanks, Mark, I'll have to look at my calendar and let you know." It wasn't as strong as it could have been, but at least she was putting him off, it only for a few minutes. "Dalton, it was just great seeing you again." She gave her most winning smile, then moved forward to kiss his cheek. "I'm running really late right now. Please excuse me." She turned and left them both standing there, watching her go.

This was great, she thought, pressing the elevator button and determinedly *not* looking back. She had left Mark hanging. He'd asked her out and she'd essentially put him on hold. That put *her* in control. Which, in turn, made her more desirable in the eyes of Mark. This was perfect.

She got on the elevator along with a crowd of strangers who probably wondered why she was smiling to herself.

Mark knocked on her open doorway just a couple of hours later. "Hey, Bonnie," he said, walking in.

She put down the report she was reviewing. "Hi again."

"Have you given any thought to dinner tonight?"

"Oh my gosh, I forgot. I'm so sorry." She actually *had* forgotten. How had *that* happened? One look at her desk answered that; she was inundated with work. "I'm swamped."

"All the more reason for you to go out and relax a little bit." He flashed a winning smile. "Come on, what do you say?"

She smiled. "Let me check my appointment book." She made a show of looking at her calendar, even though she knew she had nothing going on tonight. That is, she *thought* she had nothing going on. As it turned out, she had a dental appointment she'd completely forgotten about. She looked at Mark with an apologetic smile. "I guess tonight will be okay."

He gave a broad shrug. "Fine. Say, right after work?"

She nodded, confident with her position as the *chased* rather than the *chaser*. "Works for me."

"Okay, then." He started to leave, then grabbed the door frame and turned back. "By the way, I was hoping we could talk about the Henderson account. I have the background, of course, but I'd like your personal perspective on it. Do you have any notes on that?"

Henderson home products was one of the agency's biggest accounts. It brought in a good twenty percent of the company's annual income and only the best people were assigned to it. Bonnie had worked the account for two years herself, but had given it up when she'd accrued a number of smaller accounts. Her boss had tried to persuade her to stay on Henderson but she'd declined, offering instead to consult if anyone needed her to.

Now she wondered if Mark had been angling for help on the account all along, and she had misunderstood his intentions.

Irritation niggled at her, as she looked at him.

"Yes, I do," she said flatly.

"Terrific. Bring them along." He winked and left, and she stared after him for a few minutes before returning, a little disconcerted, to her work.

It was really crazy. Bonnie was perfectly confident in the business environment. She had no worries about her job position or security whatsoever. And normally she was pretty confident in the dating arena, too. Blue collar, white collar, older guys, younger guys, she wasn't intimidated by any of them.

Why were things so much more difficult when it came to Mark? Everything felt laborious. She had to continually remind herself that this would be worth it.

But now she was starting to wonder. Would it?

"You did it, didn't you?" Dalton asked Bonnie when she came in later that night. He was standing on a ladder fixing part of the old crown molding that had been damaged for as long as Bonnie could remember.

"Did what?" she asked, though it sounded more like "diwa" since her mouth was still numb from the Novocain the dentist had given her.

"Went out to dinner with that jerk."

She raised her eyebrows. "Now he's a jerk?"

He looked down at her, and since he was four feet up the ladder it looked even more condescending than it would have otherwise. "Yeah, he's a jerk. He asked you out to dinner right after I pretended to. Like it was a competition or something." He started down the ladder.

Bonnie watched him in surprise. "Wait a minute. You're saying he's a jerk because he asked me out when you were *pretending* to?"

Dalton nodded and put a lid on the jar of spackle he'd been working with. "That's about the size of it."

"Which means you think he's a jerk...to you. Not to me. He didn't do anything to me except ask me out, but it ticked you off because he trumped you."

"Hey. He didn't trump me. If this had been a real situation, with a real girl, I would have gotten the date."

"A *real* girl?"

"Not that you're not a real girl—"

"What *am* I?"

"You're a real girl, I mean a real woman, for sure." He raked over her with a gaze so raw that she couldn't doubt his sincerity. "Believe me, I didn't mean that, but…"

She was willing to let him squirm a little more. "But…?"

"But if I was *really* asking you out, you'd pick me over him if you had any sense."

"Because he's a jerk."

"Right."

"Because he trumped you."

"He didn't—" Dalton rolled his eyes and reached down for some sandpaper. "Forget it. So how did your night go?"

"Before he stuck the needle in me or after?"

"What?" Dalton's shock was almost amusing. He jumped off the ladder and came to Bonnie in a flash. "He stuck a *needle* in you?"

"Yes, but it's okay, he's a doctor."

Dalton opened his mouth to speak, then stopped and frowned, studying her. "What are you talking about?"

She smiled. "I didn't go out with Mark, I went to the dentist."

Dalton's facial features relaxed. "No wonder you're talking funny."

"I am?"

He nodded. "Yeah, sort of slurry. I figured you'd been drinking."

"Thanks. So you figured I was out getting drunk and being taken advantage of by Mark."

Dalton shook his head. "You can take care of yourself in a situation like that."

"Damn right I can." She started for the stairwell. "I'm exhausted, I'm going up to bed."

"Wait a minute."

She stopped and turned back to him, half expecting him to offer to join her. So why did her heart trip the way it did? "What?"

"How about making dinner next Thursday?"

She shrugged. "Fine."

He looked surprised. "You'll do it?"

"I owe you. As you're always quick to point out. So what do you want to eat this time?"

"Let's see…roast turkey, mashed potatoes, cranberry sauce—the real stuff, not the stuff that's shaped like a can—and pumpkin pie."

"Thanksgiving," Bonnie said. "Wow, how did I forget that?" Thanksgiving always gave her a pang. Her father had died when she was young, so she had managed to get through the holidays for years without feeling melancholy, but ever since losing her mother four years ago, it had been a lot harder. It probably wasn't that she'd *forgotten* Thanksgiving so much as she'd pushed it out of her mind.

"Is that still a yes?" Dalton asked. Was it her imagination or did he sound hopeful?

She wasn't sure why she hesitated. It wasn't as if she had other plans. Paula had invited her to drive down to Tampa to have Thanksgiving with her parents, but Bonnie was in the middle of an important campaign at work and couldn't afford to take the couple of extra days off that it would have required.

Maybe it was because the holidays were always a loaded situation. She was always more emotional and melancholy this time of year. That made it hard to keep up a social face in front of people.

But Dalton and Elissa weren't just 'people.' And when she entertained the idea of being with them for Thanksgiving, it made her feel more warmth than dread.

Maybe she was finally starting to be normal when it came to the holidays.

"Yes, it's a yes." Bonnie smiled, though a tremor ran through her stomach. "I told Elissa I'd teach her to cook. This is a perfect opportunity."

"Thanks," Dalton said, with sober sincerity. "Really. That'll mean a lot to her."

"It will mean a lot to me, too." Bonnie smiled and headed for the stairs again.

"By the way," Dalton called behind her. "Your ad runs in the paper tomorrow."

"For the building?"

He nodded.

"Then get ready for a lot of calls," Bonnie warned. "These places are going to fly."

Chapter Eight

"Never let him know how much you care."
—Bonnie Vaness

In fact, there was a lot of interest in the apartments. Bonnie was woken up before eight Saturday morning by the sound of people shuffling through the halls, looking at the vacant apartments on her floor.

In the afternoon, when the noise had died down, Bonnie went to Dalton's apartment to see how it had gone.

"I signed four new tenants," he said, standing in his doorway, effectively blocking the way in.

Not that Bonnie *wanted* to go in or anything, but it was only polite for him to ask. But he didn't.

"Four, huh? That's great."

"And possibly a fifth." He nodded inside, at an absolutely gorgeous woman with long chestnut hair and the kind of body normally seen only in magazine ads and on TV. "We're negotiating now."

Bonnie swallowed some discomfort she couldn't quite define. "I see."

"As a matter of fact, I've been telling Cindy about what a great place Tappen is, but if you wouldn't mind watching Elissa for a little while this evening, maybe I could take her out and show her. I think that might tip her over the edge."

Bonnie glanced at the woman's large chest and bit back a comment about it not being hard to tip her over.

"So will you do it?" Dalton asked, following Bonnie's eyes with a quizzical look.

She didn't want to. Of course, she loved Elissa and wanted to spend the time with her, but this woman, Cindy, just didn't look like the kind of person Bonnie wanted as a neighbor. So Bonnie wasn't particularly eager to go out of her way to help Dalton bring her onboard.

And she couldn't help but feel she wouldn't be doing Dalton any huge favors by helping him move her in either. She looked like the kind of woman who would break his heart and then have a long string of male visitors coming and going at all hours.

No, she didn't want this woman moving in at all.

"So can you do it?" Dalton asked.

"What time?" Bonnie asked, stalling.

"I don't know. Six?"

She noticed he *still* didn't make even the slightest move to invite her in or introduce her to his new pal.

"I've got some things to do..."

"Come on, Bonnie, you know Elissa won't be in your way. Give me a break."

And with that, she had to. There was no legitimate reason for her to refuse to help him get a date, and she had no right to discriminate against the woman just because she was beautiful and had an enormous bustline.

"All right. Send Elissa up and we'll have dinner together. In fact—" it pained her to suggest it, but she thought it would be fun for her as well as Elissa "—just tell her she can sleep over tonight. Then you can take your time with the beauty queen there." Her voice had a bit more edge to it than she had intended, but once the words were out, there was nothing she could do to get them back.

Dalton frowned and glanced back at the woman in his apartment, then back at Bonnie. "You jealous?"

"Jealous?" She gave such a sharp laugh that it drew Cindy's attention. She turned large brown eyes to Bonnie, then smiled and gave a little wave. "No," Bonnie whispered to Dalton. "I just don't think you should be abandoning your daughter so you can take some woman you don't even know out on the town."

He looked at her, amusement lighting the blue in his eyes, then a crooked smile spread across his face. "You *are* jealous."

"I'm absolutely not jealous."

"You're totally jealous."

"Just tell Elissa to come up at six," Bonnie huffed, turning on her heel. "And have a good time."

Dalton watched Bonnie stalk down the hall and tried to keep from laughing. She was jealous. He couldn't believe it. Though, looking at Cindy Payne, he had to wonder if Bonnie's jealousy had anything to do with him, or if it was simply that she didn't want another good-looking woman in the building.

"Sorry for the interruption," Dalton said, returning to the table where he and Cindy were going over the contracts. "Now, you were saying your husband will be back from Germany in a month?"

"Yes." Cindy nodded. "So I'd be needing to move in about three weeks."

"And you want a two-bedroom unit." Dalton made a mark on his notes. "I've got four left, so that shouldn't be a problem."

"Daddy?" Elissa came into the room, holding a chubby baby in her arms. "Is Liam going to be moving in?"

As soon as the baby saw his mother, he reached his arms out and made some fussy noises. Cindy went to him and lifted him from Elissa's grasp. "I think he is," she said to Elissa, patting her head. "And you would be a wonderful babysitter for him."

Elissa beamed. *"Really?"*

"You bet."

Dalton watched his daughter with pride. It was remarkable to him how relentlessly optimistic she was. She hadn't gotten that from him, that was for sure. There wasn't a cynical bone in Elissa's body.

Cindy turned back to Dalton. "So you could take a couple of hours tonight to show me around town?"

"I'd be glad to."

"Fabulous. I'll need to know the basics, like where the grocery store is and so on, but the thing I'm most concerned with is figuring out how to drive into the city for work. I start December tenth."

"We'll do a dry run tonight," Dalton suggested. "The traffic won't be too bad on a Saturday evening."

Cindy smiled. "Fabulous," she said again. "And with any luck, Liam will sleep the whole time in his car seat."

"I could take care of him here," Elissa offered.

"You're going to Bonnie's for the night," Dalton said.

Elissa's eyes lit up. "Yay! The whole night?"

He nodded. "She said to pack a bag."

"All right!"

Cindy laughed at Elissa's infectious enthusiasm. "Is Bonnie your girlfriend?" she asked him.

"He wants her to be," Elissa interjected.

Dalton shot her a look, then said to Cindy. "No, she's not. She's just an old friend."

"They've known each other since they were my age," Elissa added. "But they didn't go out."

Dalton was uncomfortable with the conversation and changed the subject. "Actually, Bonnie would be a good one to ask about commuting, since she's been doing it for years."

"I'll remember to ask," Cindy promised, gathering her things. "Thanks again for all of your help, Mr. Price."

"Call me Dalton. And it's no problem. I'm sure

you and your family will be really happy here in Tappen. When did you say the next one was due?"

Cindy patted her slightly bulging tummy. "The end of April. It's a girl."

"Can I babysit her, too?" Elissa asked eagerly.

"I'll be counting on it," Cindy said. Then to Dalton, she added, "I'll see you this evening, then. If everything goes as I expect it to, I'll be able to sign the contracts on Monday."

"It's just so typical," Bonnie fumed to Paula as they walked up and down the aisles of the Giant Eagle grocery store, picking out snacks for her night with Elissa. ""He signed four new tenants today, but this one, this *gorgeous* one, he needs to personally show around town first. She needs special attention. I'll bet you anything the rest were men."

"Why do you care?" Paula asked, picking a green grape off a bunch Bonnie had dropped into her basket. "It almost sounds like you're jealous." She popped the grape in her mouth and gave Bonnie a knowing look.

Bonnie shook her head impatiently. "That's just what he said. I am *not* jealous, I promise you. I'm just so tired of men who only go for a certain type of woman."

"You mean ones they're attracted to?"

"You should have seen her chest." Bonnie threw a box of microwave popcorn in the basket so hard it knocked some grapes off their stems. "She could use it as a flotation device. In fact, she could have been wearing a flotation device under her shirt, for all I know. I mean, is that all men think about?"

"Men or Dalton?" Paula took another grape and lifted the box of popcorn. "This has partially hydrogenated oil in it, you know."

"Men. I don't care about Dalton."

"So you said. Quite vehemently."

"I don't." Oreos landed next to the popcorn.

"Okay," Paula responded in a singsongy voice. "But for the record, I don't believe you. Ever since Dalton moved back here and into your building, you've been spending half your time either arguing with him or talking about how much he gets under your skin." She gave a smug smile. "The lady doth protest too much, methinks."

"Great time for you to remember eleventh-grade English."

"I just knew it would come in handy someday."

"It didn't. You're totally wrong."

"So you said. The lady doth—"

"So you said." Bonnie kept her voice calm and

collected. "Paula, you've known Dalton almost as long as I have. Do you seriously think I've got a thing for him?"

"You did once."

"About a thousand years ago," Bonnie scoffed.

"It wasn't that long ago." They rounded a corner to the ice-cream aisle. "What I don't get is why you're still determined to go for this boring milk-toast guy at your office when you have the hotness that is Dalton Price right in front of you."

"First of all, Mark isn't boring. Second, Dalton isn't all that hot." She thought about that for a moment. She pictured his warm liquid blue eyes, his tousled dark hair, his long dark lashes, the hooded bedroom expression he had every time he looked at her, and the way it turned her insides to Jell-O.

"That's bull hockey and you know it."

That was an argument Bonnie couldn't win, so she changed her approach. "Anyway, what does hot matter? Where will hot get you? Into bed. Maybe into a relationship for a little while, just long enough to hope that maybe *this time* things will work out. But inevitably it leads to heartbreak and wasted time."

"Wow, that's cynical."

"No, it's pragmatic. It's mature." Bonnie believed this wholeheartedly. "It's finally realizing I need to choose a man for his suitability on several important points like job, intellect, education, ambition, and so on, rather than the way he makes me tingle."

"Tingling matters."

"Not as much as the rest of it." She threw a half gallon of chocolate ice cream into the basket, then looked at what she was buying and stopped in front of the frozen vegetables to add some broccoli. "I'll trade tingling for contentment any day."

"Oh, man, not me. I'd trade contentment for tingling in a heartbeat. A rapid, pulse-pounding heartbeat."

Bonnie was surprised. "Really?"

"Absolutely. And if you're ready to give that up at your age, you're just plain crazy. For your sake I hope you win this guy over soon so you can get this asinine plan out of your system before it's too late for you to jump on the right guy and start a family." She gave a secretive smile. "Or at least a lasting affair."

Bonnie raised her eyebrows at Paula. "Is that what you've got going on?"

"*I* got a proposal."

"*What?*" Lord, where had she been? Had she honestly been so obsessed with her own problems that she'd missed such a major event in her best friend's life? "Tell me everything!"

Paula's smile widened. "Well, a sort of proposal. Seamus proposed we go away together this weekend."

Bonnie drew in a breath. "Where to?"

"Some little inn upstate." She wiggled her eyebrows like Groucho Marx. "He's already made the reservations."

"Paula, that's…" She wasn't sure. Fantastic? Or risky? She didn't want to see her friend get hurt. "That should be fun. And I guess it means you'll win our bet."

"I'm counting on it."

Bonnie smiled. This really was good news. She'd had such a bad feeling that Seamus Parker was married or something, but with Thanksgiving a week away, surely there was no way a married man could or would get away from his family for a tryst. "So is this now common knowledge at the office?"

Paula looked like she'd just stepped on a live electrical wire. "Oh, no. No way. If anyone found out, he'd lose credibility with the employees and I'd look like a bimbo." She shook her head resolutely. "I'm fine with keeping it private."

"Meaning what?" Doubt niggled at Bonnie again. "That he's the one who wants to keep it secret?"

Paula waved the notion away. "We both do. It's actually more exciting this way."

"Exciting?" It sounded just horrible to Bonnie. Nerve-racking. Almost shameful.

"That's what I'm in it for."

"And there you go," Bonnie said, pointing at her. "There, in a nutshell, is the difference between you and me. You're still after excitement. Not me. I don't *want* butterflies in my stomach. I mean, think about that. It's a hideous image. And it's a hideous feeling, really, being nervous and self-conscious all the time. I'm finished with that. Now I'm ready for stability. I want to be settled."

Paula snorted. "Settling without excitement sounds pretty bleak to me."

Bonnie sighed. Despite her impassioned argument for complacency, she occasionally indulged the same thought. Excitement was…well, *exciting.* There was, undeniably, fun in the adrenaline rush, the tripping heart, the kisses that sent flames licking through your whole body.

But that never, ever lasted.

And Dalton Price had proven, yet again, what was wrong with looking for that. Because the kind of guy who was capable of sending those shooting flames never wanted to stick around long enough to toast marshmallows over them afterward. He just moved on to the next unstruck match.

* * *

"And they lived happily ever after," Elissa announced dramatically as *The Parent Trap* rolled credits on the TV. "That was a really awesome movie."

"It's one of my favorites." Bonnie stretched, accidentally kicking aside an empty bag of microwave popcorn. It skidded across the coffee table and knocked into an empty glass with just a smidgen of homemade chocolate milk shake left in the bottom.

It had been a decadent night.

The frozen broccoli she'd bought to offset all the junk food remained unopened in the freezer.

On the other hand, there were only about ten Oreos left. If Dalton found out about this, she'd never live it down.

"Do you think a plan like that could really work to get two people together?" Elissa asked, yawning and leaning her head down on Bonnie's shoulder.

All at once, Bonnie thought of Dalton's estranged wife—Elissa's mother—and wondered if it had been a bad idea to show her *The Parent Trap* and potentially get her hopes up.

"Only if the two people really wanted to be together." She reached up and stroked Elissa's hair. "Are you thinking of someone in particular?" She rethought that and decided not to be vague. "Like your parents?"

She felt Elissa shake her head. "No, they don't want to get back together. Mommy has her career and Daddy…" Her voice was muted by fatigue. "Daddy likes someone else."

Bonnie's stomach clenched and her first impulse was to reach for the chocolate ice cream. "Cindy?"

Elissa turned and looked at her. "Who's that?"

"The woman he took out tonight."

"Oh. Mrs. Payne."

Bonnie's eyebrows shot up. "*Mrs.* Payne?" Mrs. didn't necessarily mean anything in this case. Kids always called a woman *Mrs.* even if she was a die-hard old maid. Like Bonnie.

Elissa nodded against her shoulder again. "And Liam."

"Who's Liam?"

"Mrs. Payne's baby. She's going to have another one soon, too."

"Her baby. And she's…she's going to have another one?" Bonnie groaned inwardly. No wonder Cindy had been so…generously proportioned. She was pregnant.

And apparently she *was* married.

"Her husband's in the army and he's in Germany," Elissa continued, adding "patriot" to Cindy's growing list of assets-that-made-Bonnie-feel-horrible-for-judging-her. "So Daddy took her out tonight to show her how to drive into the city for work. If it's not too far for her, she's going to rent the apartment and *I* will get to babysit."

"That's wonderful, honey," Bonnie said, cringing inwardly at what a jerk she'd been about Dalton and Cindy.

Elissa yawned and blinked sleepy eyes. "It'll be good practice. When you have a baby, someday, I can babysit for you, too."

Bonnie sighed. "Oh, honey, I don't think that's going to happen for a long, long time."

"Daddy says it's probably not going to happen at all."

Bonnie stiffened. "He did? He said I would probably never have a baby at all?"

"He said *he* probably would never have *another* baby besides me." Elissa yawned again. "I just figured if he did, it would be with you. Wouldn't it?"

Bonnie decided that Elissa must be even more exhausted than she'd thought. She had to be half dreaming, because there was no other explanation for her assuming Dalton and Bonnie would have kids together. "Your dad and I don't have that kind of relationship."

"Daddy said you do."

Bonnie raised an eyebrow, though she'd learned

quickly in this conversation to be skeptical about what Elissa said. Or at least what she meant. "Did he?"

"He said he loves you."

Bonnie's jaw dropped. "Are you sure about that?"

Elissa nodded, but her interest in the conversation had clearly dissolved. "Can I go to bed now?"

"Of course." She was so distracted, she could barely think what to tell the child to do. "Brush your teeth, then get in the bed we made up for you in my room."

"'Kay." Elissa leaned down and gave Bonnie a kiss on the cheek. "G'night."

"Goodnight, honey. Sweet dreams." Bonnie smiled and watched Elissa walk toward the bedroom in her long white flannel nightgown, looking for all the world like a character from a Victorian Christmas book.

Elissa stopped and turned back to Bonnie. "Do you think I should call Daddy and make sure he got home all right?"

Bonnie moved to the window and looked out. "There's no need. I can see his car there now. But I tell you what, maybe I'll go check on him after awhile."

Elissa nodded. "Good idea." She went back toward the bedroom, yawning loudly and making Bonnie long for the same kind of carefree relaxation.

Bonnie cleaned up the trash and the dishes, alternately talking herself into and out of going down to talk to Dalton. Eventually, when all of the dishes were done and the apartment was so pristine she couldn't possibly find another task for herself apart from going to sleep, she decided she'd go. Just to set the record straight on what their relationship was, and to make sure they both gave the right message to Elissa about it.

She tiptoed to the bedroom and peeked in on Elissa. She was sleeping soundly.

Bonnie paused in the doorway for just a moment before going to the front door, locking it securely, and going down to Dalton's.

Chapter Nine

"If you want him to know you care, you have to tell him."

—Dalton Price

"What on earth have you been telling your daughter about us?" Bonnie asked as soon as Dalton opened the door.

Dalton, standing at his doorway in sweatpants with no shirt on, looked confused, then glanced behind Bonnie. "Where is she?"

"She's asleep in my room," Bonnie said, pushing

her way past him into the apartment. "Is that okay? To leave her there?"

He watched her come in, then pushed the door closed. "Yeah. She's not that young. Besides, the security lock in the lobby is on."

"That's what I figured." She turned to face him in the half light and leaned against the back of the couch. "Anyway, I told her I'd come down here and check on you."

"What do you mean check on me?"

"She wanted to be sure you got home all right, that's all. I told her your car was out there."

He gave a sly smile. "So now you're spying on me?"

"Come off it. It's not like you were on a date."

"But if I *was* on a date, *then* you'd be spying on me?"

"That's not what I meant."

He crossed his arms in front of him, and the shadows cast by the one weak light that was on in the room called her attention to his muscular torso. "What did you mean?"

"This is all beside the point, Dalton," Bonnie said, willing her attention *away* from his torso. "The point is that she thinks we're going to have babies together. You and me."

"What? Did you tell her that?"

"Of course I didn't tell her that. What's wrong

with you?" From the looks of it, nothing was wrong with him. And Bonnie could have kicked herself for having thoughts about his body and his gorgeous mouth at a serious time like this.

"So where'd she get that idea?"

"I don't know. That's why I'm down here, asking the guy who's raising her." She looked at him pointedly. "She also thinks you love me. Why would she think something like that?"

He looked startled for a moment, then frowned, and gestured toward the couch. "Sit down. Want a beer?"

"No, thanks."

He went to the kitchen, his muscular frame silhouetted briefly by the light of the refrigerator and grabbed two anyway. He came back and tossed one to Bonnie before twisting the top off the other one and taking a long swig. "About me loving you—"

Something surged through Bonnie's chest.

"—we were talking about love the other night after she went to Sunday school. She asked me if we were really supposed to love everyone, and I tried to explain what the teacher had meant, but Elissa had to go down a list of people to make sure I loved them all."

"And I was on your list?" Bonnie smiled. "I'm on your love list?"

Dalton's face colored. "Come on, don't make this

harder than it is. You know what I'm saying. It was the whole God-loves-everyone and God-is-within-us-all lesson."

Bonnie laughed. "Don't worry, I know what you mean. I think I remember being puzzled by that particular concept myself when I was about Elissa's age. Probably from the same Sunday school teacher, now that I think about it."

He nodded. "Me too."

"Oh, yeah, I forgot you were there too."

"That's because I was usually banished to the hall for being disruptive."

She smirked. "Your butt spent a lot of time on linoleum between Sunday school and regular school."

He drank from his beer and shrugged. "Someone had to be the bad kid."

"We, the good kids of the world, thank you."

He looked at her. "Elissa's a good kid."

"Yes, she is. She's a great kid."

He took another swig then wiped his mouth with the back of his hand. "She deserves more than she's got."

Bonnie went to him and put a hand on his shoulder. "Don't say that, Dalton. She's got so much. She's so happy. Really. You ought to be damn proud of yourself."

His gaze was even, but inscrutable, "She saw her

mom on TV the other day. Just for a minute. She was playing a waitress on some stupid sitcom so she had like two lines, but, given what she said to you, it must have affected Elissa more than I thought."

"Is that all she sees of her mother?" Bonnie's heart ached immediately. "The occasional moment on TV?"

"Yup." He drank again. "That's about the size of it."

"Oh." Bonnie twisted the top off the beer bottle he'd tossed to her. It hissed and foamed slightly at the neck. "That's really sad." A moment passed. "But surely that wouldn't lead to some delusion about you and me getting together, would it? It doesn't exactly follow." A dribble of beer ran down onto her hand and she wiped it on her jeans.

"No," he agreed. "But she's been talking about it a lot lately. "Not about us having kids together or anything, but about having you over more, or how great it was when you came over and cooked dinner." He blew air into his cheeks, then sighed heavily. "All that maternal stuff you do. Or at least maternal compared to her mother."

"Should I stop?"

"No, no," he said quickly. "Please. No. It's still good for her to have you around. It's good for her to have a woman to look up to and pal around with sometimes. You can talk to her about things I can't."

He shook his head ruefully. "You definitely shouldn't back off. Look, I'll just talk to her, set her straight. It won't be a problem."

"You sure?"

"Sure I'm sure." But he didn't look sure. He studied the beer bottle in his hand, then turned his gaze back to Bonnie. "So did you two have a good time tonight?"

"Yes, it was great. We watched *The Parent Trap*."

"What's that?"

"Oh, you know. That old movie with Brian Keith and Maureen O'Hara."

He looked blank.

Bonnie shook her head. "Men. Honestly. It's one of the greatest movies of all time."

He chuckled. "Wonder how I missed it then."

"What about your night?" she asked. "How'd everything go with Cindy?"

He shrugged. "Okay. I think she's going to rent the place. And she might be talking to you about commuting into the city for work, so if she does, be nice."

"Why *wouldn't* I be nice?"

"Well, you were a little snippy when you saw her here earlier."

Bonnie clicked her tongue against her teeth. "That is *not* true. I was just…tired."

He snorted. "Yeah, jumping to conclusions can be exhausting."

She gave him a withering look. "Jumping to conclusions? About what?"

"About me and Cindy. You thought there was something going on. It was written all over your face."

She instinctively raised a hand to her cheek. "What do I care what you do?"

"Funny you should ask. I was wondering the same thing." He set his beer down and walked closer to her in the dimly lit apartment. "What *do* you care?" He stopped just a couple of feet before her, facing her like a boxer facing off in the ring.

"I don't," she said weakly. Suddenly her mouth felt dry and she took a sip of the beer. It was warm.

He took a step closer.

She could practically feel the heat pulsating from his body to hers. "No?"

"No." Never had a *no* from her lips sounded more like a *yes*. "What you do is your business."

"Yeah?"

"Yeah," she breathed. Her palms felt slick. She set her bottle down on the end table so she didn't drop it.

He stood still before her and she found herself taking the next step toward him.

What was she *doing?* This was insane. Dalton

was magnetism personified—she wasn't approaching him because she *wanted* to, she was approaching him because she couldn't *stop*.

"I'd better get back to Elissa." She took a quick, steadying breath and started to walk around him.

But he stopped her, putting a hand to her arm. "Wait."

"What?" she asked in a rush of breath.

Their faces were now just inches apart.

"Don't go," he said softly.

"Why not?" she whispered.

He looked at her for a long moment before saying, "I can't give you one good reason to stay."

She swallowed. "Then I'd better go." But she didn't move. Her body tingled at his proximity. His mouth was so close to hers that she wouldn't have had to take so much as a single step forward in order to kiss him. All she'd have to do was lean just a little bit....

But she couldn't. She wouldn't.

He, on the other hand, did.

With a hunger normally reserved for hormone-driven teenagers, he took one bold step forward and scooped her into his arms, holding her hard against him while his mouth moved tenderly over hers, igniting fires in places she hadn't felt heat for years.

A tingle tripped down her spine and settled deep, burning steadily within her. When Dalton's tongue touched hers, the flame flared. She pulled Dalton closer, pressing her hands against the lean, muscled physique that she had thought about so many times over the years.

He traced his hands slowly down her back, sending shivers of mingled pleasure and desire shuddering through her. When he pulled her closer against himself, she could tell that he wanted her as much as she wanted him.

It would have been so easy to take his hand and wordlessly lead him into the bedroom to satiate the desire that had hungered within her for so long. They were adults, free to do what they wanted. One night of pleasure didn't commit them to a lifetime together. It didn't have to mean anything deep. It didn't have to mean anything at all.

Except, for Bonnie, it did.

Much as her body wanted him within her—*now!*—her heart knew that she couldn't make a move like that without at least the intention of making the relationship last longer than a night. She wasn't a one-night-stand kind of girl. Never had been. Not on purpose, anyway.

And Dalton Price was the only one who ever made

her think about giving in to that foolish impulse. But not tonight. If she gave in, it would blow everything she was trying to achieve with Mark. It would taint the integrity of her plan.

To say nothing of how incredibly difficult it would make it for her to live here, in Dalton's building, seeing him every day. She knew herself well enough to know that she'd have a hard time acting casual with him if they did this.

Again.

"What are we *doing?*" Bonnie pulled back.

"We're—kissing. What do you mean what are we doing?"

She narrowed her eyes at him. "You're testing me, aren't you?"

He looked flummoxed. "*Testing* you?"

"My loyalty to Mark." She knew how stupid it sounded even as she said it, but it was the best she could come up with on the spur of the moment. She had to remind herself—and Dalton—that her intentions lay elsewhere. That she was *not* going to fall into this with Dalton.

"You're not even going out with Mark!"

"Not yet. But that's just the point. I'm supposed to be holding out for him. You're supposed to be *helping* me get him. This, you and me—" she scanned a pointing finger between them "—cannot happen."

His mouth curled into a sexy smile. "It happened once."

She nodded, still feeling flushed. "Which is one of the many reasons it cannot happen again." Her heart pounded. She wanted it to happen again. At least, her *body* wanted it to happen again.

Her mind was completely against it.

"To be honest with you, Bon, that's one of the reasons I'd *like* for it to happen again."

Something inside of her weakened. "Really?" Had it meant more to him than he'd let on? Was it possible that he'd harbored some long-standing unresolved feelings, just like she had? "I'm surprised to hear that, Dalton, I really am."

"Why?"

"Because I didn't know you'd ever even thought about it."

"I have lately."

She swallowed. "Oh?"

"Yeah. All this talk about your dream man, Mike or whatever his name is—"

"Mark."

"I can't help but be aware of the possibility of…you know, bad memories."

Now she was completely confused. "What are you talking about? What bad memories?"

"Well, you and I…" He cleared his throat. "You know. I was nineteen or something at the time. What guy wouldn't like the chance to—" he shrugged "—give a better performance."

Bonnie could have slapped him. "Prove yourself, you mean. Prove your manhood."

He did, at least, have the grace to look a little bit embarrassed. "I guess you could put it that way."

"God, you're a jerk."

He spread his arms wide. "Hey, what did I do?"

"No, no, *I'm* a jerk. For just a moment there I actually thought that what happened between us might have meant a *little* something to you, but, no." She threw her hands in the air. "I should have known it was all about your ego. It always is with good-looking guys."

He smiled. "You think I'm good-looking?"

"Not anymore," she answered crisply. "I'm going home." She pushed past him without waiting for a response.

"I hope this doesn't mean Thanksgiving's off."

She turned and gave him a dry look. "I don't think the United States will call off Thanksgiving because of this, no."

"I mean you coming here for Thanksgiving." The cocky look was gone, replaced by one of complete earnestness. "Elissa's really counting on it."

There was nothing Bonnie would have liked more than to tell Dalton where he could stuff his turkey, but she knew he was right; Elissa *was* looking forward to it. There was no way on earth Bonnie was going to let that child down, no matter what. "I'll be here," Bonnie said. "Not for you, but for Elissa."

He splayed his arms. "Fair enough."

She shook her head wearily and started to leave.

"Bon."

She stopped and turned back to face him. "What?"

A long moment trembled between them.

"It did mean something to me." She saw him swallow. "I know you probably don't believe that, but it's the truth."

She was stunned by the emotion that filled her. Feelings of rejection mingled with desire and remembered passion. She pressed her lips together, not trusting herself to respond. Instead, she just looked at him for a moment, scrutinizing his face for signs of sincerity—or a punch line—and wasn't sure what she saw. "Honestly, I don't even know what to believe anymore," she said.

He gave a humorless laugh. "Does anyone? That's real life, sweetheart."

For the first time that night she knew with absolute certainty that Dalton meant exactly what he said. And the sentiment made her unutterably sad. Suddenly all she wanted was to go back to her apartment, to a dippy old romantic movie and to the sweet, sleeping child who still believed in happily ever after.

Chapter Ten

"Sometimes it's better to be lonely than sorry."
—Bonnie Vaness

When Bonnie got back to her apartment, the telephone was ringing. She ran to grab it, so it wouldn't wake Elissa, but it stopped just as she picked up the receiver. She replaced it and noticed that the answering machine light was blinking. The indicator said there were five messages.

The first two were hang-ups, three minutes apart. The third was an almost unrecognizable-sounding

Paula. "Call me. I don't care what time. I'm at home."
It sounded like she was sick or crying.

Immediately followed another hang-up, but after
that, time-stamped ten minutes after she'd left the
first, Paula left another message. "Bonnie, damn it,
where *are* you? If you're there, pick up. I *really* need
to talk to you. *Please.*"

Her tone was alarming. Bonnie hurried to the bedroom, took a quick glance at the still-sleeping Elissa,
then closed the door quietly and was about to pick
up the phone to call Paula when it rang.

"What's wrong?" Bonnie asked, not even bother-
ing to find out who it was first. She knew.

Paula answered with something unintelligible,
punctuated by sobs.

Bonnie tried to decipher it. "Someone got *hit?*
What are you talking about? Slow down and tell me
what's going on."

"I *said* he's *married,* the son of a bitch."

"Oh." Bonnie closed her eyes for a moment and
sank down onto the nearest seat. "Oh, no. Oh, Paula,
honey, I'm so sorry."

Paula sniffed loudly. "I *hate* him."

"I don't blame you. I hate him, too."

"But that's not all. It—it gets worse." Paula dissolved into another fit of uncontrolled sobs.

Bonnie's heart lurched. No. It couldn't be. Please, please, she prayed. *Please* don't let Paula be pregnant. "Stay right where you are. Don't move. I'm coming over." She said it loud enough so that Paula would hear her over her own crying. "Hold on, okay? I'll be there in fifteen minutes."

Paula drew a shuddering breath. "Bon, you don't have to…yes, you do. Thanks." She sniffed again, then added, quickly, "Hurry."

Bonnie hung up the phone and immediately dialed Dalton.

He answered the phone just the way she had five minutes earlier. "What's wrong?"

"It's Paula." Bonnie's hands were shaking. "She's upset and she needs me to come over. Should I bring Elissa down to you or do you want to come up?"

"Don't worry about it," Dalton said quickly. "I'll come up and get her."

His voice brought a measure of calm to Bonnie's nerves. "Thanks, Dalton," she said, before she realized the line was already dead.

One minute later he was at the door. "What's going on?" he asked, as Bonnie hurried to dig a coat out of the closet. "Is Paula all right?"

"Man troubles," she said, tossing aside a fleece wrap she hadn't worn for ten years. "Nothing serious."

"I hope you didn't tell Paula it was nothing serious."

Bonnie turned and gave him the dead eye. "Of course I didn't. She's heartbroken. She needs support. I'm just saying…"

"That most men are worthless slobs," Dalton finished for her. "I got it."

"Good." She pulled her long L.L. Bean coat out of a pile in the back of the closet and turned to face him.

He didn't take the bait. Didn't joke back. Instead he said, "You're wrong about men, Bonnie Vaness. You're cynical and bitter, and I kind of understand why, but still you're wrong to make generalizations about all men." Two heartbeats crossed between them. "And about me."

She geared herself up to make the most insensitive and untrue statement of her life. "Dalton, I don't even think about you."

He looked at her for a moment, but instead of the insult she had anticipated, she saw only disbelief.

"Sure." The way he said it could have been interpreted at least five different ways. "Look," he continued, after a moment, "why don't you take my truck? You'll get to Paula's a lot faster." He reached into his pocket and pulled out a brass key ring with four keys on it and tossed it in Bonnie's direction.

She caught it. The keys were still warm from his

body heat and she curled her fingers around them and held on tight. "Thanks, Dalton. I—" She took a short breath. It would be stupid for her to apologize, to admit she might be wrong about him. After that kiss, such an admission could lead to anything. "I appreciate it."

Paula greeted Bonnie at the door with a bottle of tequila and breath that could start an explosion if someone lit a match. "You didn't need to come," she said, but she was so stuffed up from crying that it sounded like she said *oo didund deed do gum.* Then she raised her eyebrows and the bottle simultaneously and asked, "Wanna drink?"

"This," Bonnie said, taking the bottle from her, "isn't going to help one bit."

"It's already helping."

"Yeah, for about ten minutes. Then comes the big ugly crash. How much have you had?"

"I dunno. One, two shots." But she counted six on her fingers. "I want one more."

"Forget it." Bonnie led Paula into the living room and gently pushed her into a seated position on the couch. "Sit here for a minute. I'm getting you some coffee."

"I'll puke."

"Okay, then I'm getting you some cola. Got any?"

"Under the sink." Paula gestured in the direction of the bathroom but Bonnie knew she meant it was in the kitchen.

"I lied," Paula wailed from the other room.

Bonnie poked her head up. "About what?"

"I don't want excitement. This is the price you pay for excitement. I want to be content. I want a boring accountant who drives a sensible little car and lives in the suburbs who will love and respect me and never leave me and not be m-m-married."

"Amen!"

"I don't feel so good."

"Hang on, I'll be right there." Bonnie looked under the sink, then in the cabinet next to the one under the sink and found a two-liter bottle of diet cola. She doubted it had the stomach-calming powers of regular cola, but at least it had the caffeine. And it *didn't* contain alcohol. She dropped a few ice cubes into a glass and poured the flat soda over it. It would have to do, at least for now.

She took it back to Paula, who drank as if it were the first water she'd had after ten days in the desert.

"Thanks, Bon," she said, biting down on an ice cube. "You're a real pal."

Bonnie sat next to her and put her hand on Paula's shoulder. "You want to tell me what happened?"

"What's to tell? I thought he might be The One and instead he's a lying, manipulative son of a bitch with a wife, two-point-five kids, and a house with a garage in the suburbs. The house is in the burbs," she hiccuped, "not just the garage."

"Poor baby." Bonnie drew Paula close and stroked her hair while she cried. "I'm so sorry."

"His wife's probably content, you know."

"If she is, she's wrong."

"At least she's safe. At least he's not going to dump her." Paula leveled a blood-red gaze on Bonnie. "He made that absolutely clear."

"Ugh." Bonnie held the cola up for Paula to take another sip.

She did, along with a couple of convulsive breaths. "But that isn't a-a-all. It gets so much worse."

Bonnie braced herself for it. The moment was here. Paula was going to tell her she was pregnant and Bonnie was going to commit to helping her raise the child, and she was going to spend the rest of her life as one of "those two weird old ladies who live in the big old Victorian house on Crabapple Street."

"What else?" Bonnie asked, as gently as she could.

"He—he—" Paula lost it again. "I can't even believe it."

"Can't believe what? What did he do? He abandoned you in your time of need?"

"You could say that."

"That's what I was afraid of." Bonnie gave Paula a squeeze. "Don't worry, I'll help you raise it."

Paula drew back and looked at Bonnie, through tequila- and tear-reddened eyes, like she was crazy. "Help me raise what?"

Bonnie gave her best, placid Mother Mary smile, even though she was panicking inside. "The baby."

Paula's jaw dropped. *"Baby?"*

"Yes…no?"

"What, do you think I'm an idiot? I'm not pregnant!"

"You're not?" Relief flooded through Bonnie like adrenaline.

"No!"

"Then what is it? What's the thing he did that's *worse* than lying to you and being married?"

"He *fired* me." Paula shook her head and even managed a brief chuckle. "He didn't knock me up. I do take precautions, you know."

Bonnie looked into Paula's eyes. "You're not pregnant?"

"No!"

"You're sure?"

Paula gave her a condescending look. "If I am, you can look for a huge star in the north sky on December twenty-fifth."

Bonnie narrowed her eyes.

"Well, okay, it wouldn't be exactly *immaculate* but it's not possible. Believe me, I take care of myself." Paula sniffled. "I'm not believing any man who's claiming he's been snipped and we don't need to worry."

"Oh. Okay. Good." Bonnie was flummoxed. "I'm glad to hear that. But…he fired you? As in, took away your livelihood?"

"Bingo."

"And you're unemployed?" Bonnie was rapidly growing incensed. "Because of that jerk?"

"You've got it."

"This is outrageous. He can't do that!"

"He can and he did. He's the boss."

"There are laws to protect you from this kind of thing, you know," Bonnie said, ready to check the yellow pages for lawyers' phone numbers. "He can't get away with this."

"I don't want to make waves."

Bonnie looked at her. "You don't want to make waves."

"No."

"You're unemployed. You can't afford *not* to make waves."

Paula took another sip of the awful flat cola, then looked at Bonnie. "I can't go back to work there. Sure, maybe a slick lawyer could get me my job back, but then everyone would know that I—slept with him. And he's married. And I'm an idiot."

"You are *not* an idiot. You're a normal person who believes a guy when he says he's not married. Especially a guy you work with, who you'd think would be careful about…" A terrible thought occurred to her. "Do you think he'd planned to sack you the whole time?"

"Sack as in fire, or sack as in—"

"Fire."

Paula shrugged. "I don't know. I don't care. I just hate him." She lost herself in tears again.

Bonnie put her arm around her friend and just held her while she cried. It went on for quite some time, during which Bonnie rocked her gently and occasionally whispered, "It'll be all right," even though she knew that, to Paula, it seemed like things would never be all right again.

Finally Paula calmed down and fell asleep. When her breathing was steady and even, Bonnie carefully extracted herself, laying Paula on the sofa and covering her with the afghan her grandmother had crocheted.

She crept to the phone, took it off the cradle, and went into the bedroom to call Dalton.

"I'm sorry to call so late," she began.

"I'm up."

"Did you get Elissa back to her bed all right?"

"She didn't even wake up."

Bonnie imagined him carrying the child down the hall in his powerful arms, being careful not to wake her, and something in her stirred to life. Something that really needed to be stopped. "Good," she said. "Listen, I have to ask you a favor. Can I stay over here tonight?"

"Since when do you need my permission?"

Bonnie smiled to herself. "Since I have your truck."

"Oh, yeah. Sure, no, it's no problem. I don't need it tonight."

"Thanks." She sat down on Paula's bed, not quite ready to hang up yet. "I guess you're right, I *did* underestimate you. A little."

There was a hesitation before he said, "I think your implication was that all men, including myself, were scum."

She smiled. "Tomato, tomahto."

"No, no. I want to hear you admit that you were completely wrong about me." There was laughter in his voice.

Bonnie settled back against Paula's pillow, enjoying herself even while she knew she shouldn't be. "I didn't say I was wrong about *you*," she teased.

"You're totally wrong about me."

"You don't even know what I think of you."

"Then tell me what you think of me."

She hesitated, a million things running through her mind. "You don't want to know what I think of you."

"Yes, I do."

Because there was darkness and distance between them, she couldn't tell just how he meant that. Was he serious, or just baiting her for more ribbing?

It was impossible to say.

So she chose her words carefully. "Well, in high school, I thought you were one hot tamale. But who didn't?"

"Come on."

"I'm serious!" She couldn't believe he didn't know this already. "All the girls were after you."

"Not you."

Her face felt hot in the darkness of Paula's bedroom. "How do you know?"

"Because I was chasing you and you never once looked back and saw me."

"Oh, come *on*, Dalton, how dumb do you think I am?"

"I mean it." He sounded as if he did. "I wanted you more than anything."

She cleared her throat gently. "Well, if I recall correctly, you eventually got me. And my phone wasn't exactly ringing off the hook afterwards." The silence that followed was so long that Bonnie eventually had to ask, "Are you still there?"

"I'm here."

"Too chicken to respond?" Her heart pounded. She didn't feel nearly as casual about this as she was trying to sound, but it was the first time she'd ever had the chance to call him on this and she wasn't going to let it go.

"You wanna play chicken?" he asked. "You didn't call me either."

"It was up to you!"

"Why was it up to me?"

"Because…" It was on the tip of her tongue to say *because you're the guy* but she knew that would come across wrong. "Because you knew I wanted you to."

"No, I didn't." He said it quietly. Plainly.

For a moment, she was at a loss. "What, you thought I didn't want you to call?"

"You never said you did."

"Bull—" Had she? She wasn't sure. "Whether I did or not, it would have been the honorable thing."

"Yeah, well, ditto."

"Ditto?" she repeated so loudly she was afraid she might have woken Paula. "That's manure and you know it. It's not up to the girl to call afterwards, it's up to the guy." There. She'd said it. Politically incorrect as it might be, she'd said it.

"How do you figure that? It was my impression we were in it together."

She scoffed. "You could hardly say the stakes were the same for each of us."

"And what the hell is that supposed to mean?"

"That you didn't give anything by being with me. It wasn't a compromise of any sort for you, it was just another conquest."

He was silent.

"So you admit it?" she asked, hating how shrill she sounded.

"I was nineteen, Bonnie. And an idiot. And on top of that, I figured, rightly, that if you wanted to talk to me, you'd call."

"Which, by your logic, means you didn't want to talk to *me*."

"No, it's…complicated."

"Please."

There was a long silence before he said, "I've got to hang up now, Bon. I think I hear Elissa."

"You're making that up."

"We'll talk tomorrow." His voice was quiet but it was clear that compromise was not an option. He was finished with the conversation. "Keep the truck as long as you need to, and I'll see you when you get back."

Chapter Eleven

"Make him think about you, even when you're not there. It'll drive him nuts."

—Dalton Price

"My head is killing me," Paula announced, not surprisingly, the next morning.

Bonnie handed her a disgusting concoction that was not unlike a Bloody Mary made with tequila instead of vodka. Hair of the dog. The recipe had called for a raw egg to be swirled into the mixture, but that just seemed unnecessarily cruel. "Here. I have it on good authority this will help you feel better."

Paula took a skeptical sniff. "Is this from more of your Internet research?"

"Be glad you have a friend who will do that for you. Now drink up."

Paula drank the disgusting mixture, then groaned and plunked onto the sofa. "Don't *ever* let me do that again."

"You were already done doing it by the time I got here!"

"Next time get here sooner." She frowned and looked at Bonnie. "Where were you, anyway? I called you like five hundred times."

"I was at Dalton's."

Paula wasn't one to blithely accept a statement like that without question. "Oh? Doing what?"

"What do you mean, doing what? We were just talking." But the flush that burned her cheeks told a different story and it was clear that Paula could see that.

"So now you've got two guys on the line. Dalton *and* that guy at work?"

"Wait a minute, who said I have anyone on the line? I've got *no one* on the line, and I'm starting to think I never will."

"Sure," Paula snorted. "Throw me a bone."

"I'm serious, Paula. You know there's nothing going on between Dalton and me. The whole idea is absurd." She thought of the kiss they'd shared just hours ago, the memory of his lips on hers, his arms around her...she felt warm all over.

Paula groaned again. "God, you're stupid."

"Just what is that supposed to mean?"

"Oh, you know damn well what it means." She put a hand to her forehead and leaned back. "Now be a true friend and get me a cool, wet washcloth, would you? I've got some healing to do. Then I need to find a new job."

Okay, Bonnie acknowledged to herself as she drove Dalton's old Toyota back home. Maybe she did know what Paula meant. Or at least she could peg at least one or two appropriate meanings onto it.

Dalton was really attractive. Magnetically attractive. Even now, sitting in his truck, she could feel her body respond to...what? His scent, lingering in the air? His touch, fingerprinted on the steering wheel? The sort of DNA bits that only a forensics specialist could find? Bonnie couldn't say what it was, but there was something of Dalton here that made her pulse drum just a little bit faster.

And it really irritated her because she didn't *want* to be attracted to Dalton anymore. She'd spent far too long on that dead-end road. In fact, her new plan with Mark Ford was a not-indirect result of that very thing. Chemistry had failed her. Attraction was an illusion. And it only led to too many hours hoping for the phone to ring, and too many days feeling defeated and heartbroken.

Bonnie wasn't going to do that again.

So, she thought, tightening her hands on the steering wheel, she was going to move forward with her plan to win the handsome, successful, and, okay, bland Mark Ford. She'd take bland contentment over red-hot heartache anytime.

When she got back to the apartment building, Dalton was nowhere to be seen. So she pocketed his keys and went up to her apartment for a much-needed nap.

Dalton woke up late Sunday morning, after dreams that had left him groggy, yet fitful and uncomfortable. He couldn't remember them, but he knew that Bonnie had been in them. He wasn't entirely sure why they left him feeling so disconcerted, but he had a pretty good idea. Bonnie herself left him feeling disconcerted lately—why would dreams about her be any different?

He hauled himself out of bed and found Elissa talking on the phone in the kitchen. As soon as she saw him, she cupped her hand over the receiver and excitedly asked, "Can I sleep over at Susan's? Please? Her mom can pick me up."

Dalton blinked and shook his fuzzy head. "Sure. If you want to."

"Yes!" Elissa pumped a small fist in the air, a gesture he recognized as an occasional one of his own. "I can do it!" she said into the receiver. "My dad says it's fine." She listened, then looked at the clock while her friend spoke. "Okay. I'll wait out front." She hung up and told Dalton that Susan's mother would be picking her up in half an hour.

"All right, just let me get dressed and start some coffee and I'll wait downstairs with you." He threw some coffee into the automatic brewer and went back to the bedroom for a quick shower.

As the minutes wore on, the feeling of his dreams dissolved, and when he got back to the kitchen and poured his first cup of joe, he felt considerably better. That feeling lasted all the way through the trip downstairs, saying goodbye to Elissa, and closing the door behind her.

Then Bonnie appeared. She'd come to get her mail a day late and when she saw Dalton, she looked as surprised as he felt, although the fact that they'd run into each other was nothing surprising. It happened every day.

But he didn't have dreams about her every day.

And she didn't look as if she knew it every day.

"Hey," he said.

"Hey." She swallowed and went past him to the mailbox. "I've got your keys upstairs. When I went to your door, no one answered."

"I was asleep. And I've told Elissa not to answer the door herself unless she knows who it is."

Bonnie nodded. "Well, you want to come up with me and get them? Or just wait here, I'll go get them and bring them back."

"You don't need to do that, I'll just come get them from you. I'm on my way up anyhow." He ushered her toward the stairs. "Come on, let's go."

She went without question, neither talking as they climbed the steps up to the third floor. When they got to Bonnie's apartment, she pulled her keys out of her pocket with a hand that shook slightly, and opened the door. "Come on in," she said.

Dalton caught the door as it swung closed and stepped in behind her.

"The keys are in here, I'll just be a second," Bonnie said, disappearing into the kitchen.

Dalton stood awkwardly in the vestibule, looking around. The place looked the same as it ever had, but suddenly it *felt* different. For some reason, he suddenly felt like an illicit visitor, a person who didn't belong and who might be in trouble if he was discovered.

"Now, that's strange," Bonnie said, coming out of the kitchen. "I could have sworn I left them on the counter."

"You lost my keys?"

"No! No, they were on the counter and…" She looked puzzled, and glanced behind her as if some prankster might jump out from behind the curtains, jingling Dalton's key chain. "And now they're not." She frowned.

"It's not like this is a huge place," Dalton said. "They couldn't have just disappeared. Where else did you go? Did you check the bathroom?"

"I didn't take your keys to the bathroom," she answered impatiently.

He shrugged. "Did you check? I find the damnedest things in the bathroom—"

"Too much information." She held up a hand. "Trust me, they're not there."

"Ahh. So this is some kind of trick to get me to wait around here while you look." Dalton smiled, not thinking, for even a moment, that she'd take him seriously.

"I did not!" she objected, with some vigor.

"Calm down, I was just kidding."

"I'd hope so."

"Well, I was."

"Good, because it's not like I'm looking for excuses to keep you around."

"Who said you were?"

Her face flushed pink. "I'm just saying, I didn't."

"What's that Shakespeare line about the lady protesting too much?"

Bonnie shot him a look. "Have you been talking to Paula?"

"About Shakespeare?"

"About *anything*," she said impatiently. "About me."

Dalton looked at her for a moment in disbelief, then said, "No, I haven't been talking to anyone about you. But the way you're acting, I'm thinking maybe I should."

She smiled, and it was completely disarming. "I didn't mean to snap. It's just that Paula said something just like that the other day. It's not often that I get two *Hamlet* references in one week."

Dalton considered that, distilling her sentence down to its essence. "Paula thought you were objecting too much about your feelings for me?"

There it was again, that unmistakable pinkening of Bonnie's cheeks. "No. Not about you. She was talking about something else entirely. No, no, it wasn't you." She cleared her throat in a way he thought sounded nervous. "No, I just thought it was strange that two people should make the same sort of reference this week, that's all. But they say if the idea is flying around the universe…" She didn't finish. She looked like she was out of gas.

"Gotcha," Dalton said, to let her off the hook.

She looked relieved. "Good."

"So," he said, thinking even as he said it that he had some sort of follow-up, but he didn't.

"So."

"Got any other ideas?"

Her eyes were warm orbs of blue, and at first she didn't seem to comprehend his meaning. "About Shakespeare?"

He kept his smile in check. "*Do* you have any other ideas about Shakespeare?" He took a step forward, and couldn't stop himself from taking her hands in his. "Or about anything else?"

She swallowed visibly. "I've got a lot of ideas."

He didn't let go of her hands. "Tell me one."

"You don't want to know."

"Yes, I do."

"I don't want to say."

"Do it anyway."

She didn't take her hands from his, but instead stood before him, looking into his eyes like a caged animal. Partly frightened, partly challenging. Not backing away at all. "Sometimes, Dalton, I get the idea that you're trying to seduce me."

He raised his brows. "Yeah?"

"Yeah."

"And if that were true—and I'm not saying it is—would that really be a problem?"

She nodded.

"Why is that?"

"Because you're bad for me, Dalton Price."

Something about the way she said it invited him to take a step closer. "Bad in a bad way or in a good way?" he asked her in a low voice.

She took a quick breath, keeping her eyes on his, then shook her head. "I'm not sure."

Now it was as if his body were acting on its own, independent of anything he willed or she said. He put an arm around her waist and pulled her closer. "Then it can't be too bad, can it?"

She pressed her lips together and blinked before saying, "I don't know. I've been trying not to think about it."

"You mean you've been trying not to think about me?"

"Yes." She nodded. "I've been trying not to think

about you. Because you, Dalton, just confuse matters. You always have."

He rested his other hand on her hip. "Then you and I have something in common, don't we?"

Chapter Twelve

"The right touch can make up for a lot of unspoken words."

—Dalton Price

For a moment, Bonnie couldn't breathe. She couldn't move. And she definitely couldn't move away from Dalton's touch, even while the harpy voice in her mind told her to run.

Wordlessly, he bent down and lowered his mouth to hers.

His lips grazed lightly at first, like he was testing

her. She suspended her reaction for just a moment before giving in to the pull and leaning against him.

She looked up into his eyes and their breath mingled between them.

Then Dalton gave the briefest smile and lowered his mouth onto hers, hungry. Insistent. It was as if they were both making up for years of lost time. She could have fallen into this kiss forever. Waves of dizzying pleasure swirled through not just her body, but her heart. Her spirit.

Something about Dalton got to her. It always had. And as much as she tried to resist it—indeed, as much as she knew she *had* to resist it—sometimes it was so compelling that she was absolutely powerless in the face of it.

This was one of those times.

His mouth moved effortlessly across hers, like a practiced musician performing a simple, yet beautiful, scale by rote. When his tongue touched hers, a jolt of desire shuddered through her and she traced her hands up his arms and pulled him closer to her. But she couldn't get him close enough to satisfy the growing ache deep within her.

Patiently, Dalton ran his hand down to the small of her back, resting there in a quiet, yet powerful pose while his mouth worked on removing her resistance.

"Where is Elissa?" she asked, holding on to the last piece of driftwood that could stop her from drowning in this sea.

"She's gone to a friend's house. She'll be gone all night."

Something deep within Bonnie trilled. "All night?"

Dalton kissed her, then smiled against her mouth. "All night. Got any plans?"

"Just a few ideas," she said, smiling back. "But I'm not so sure they're *good* ideas."

His fingertips slid to the top of her cotton underwear. "I'm sure they are."

She gasped at his touch. "Yeah, well, I'm not sure your judgment is all it could be."

"I have other talents."

A pulse throbbed in her core, like a hypnotic jungle beat, willing him to keep going, to keep touching her, to never ever stop.

It was as if he understood that primal call, just as she did. He moved on steadily, confidently. There was no question of whether he would stop, and there was no question of whether she wanted him to. She didn't.

He slipped his hands under her shirt, his fingers tripping lightly along the bare skin above her bra.

Bonnie rose in response, with heightened awareness of his touch and anticipation of his moves that bordered on desperation.

As Dalton's lips moved against hers and his tongue probed gently in her mouth, Bonnie felt the ache that had existed within her for far too long start to demand satisfaction. She didn't care if it was wrong, she didn't care if it was stupid, her soul had a question that needed Dalton's answer.

Bonnie let go of her inhibitions. She had no choice. The desire within her was so deep as to not be denied.

His touch remained warm on her breast, playing at the nipple until her breath came in short, urgent bursts. When she couldn't stand it any longer, she reached for the button of his jeans and twisted it free, pulling the zipper apart with two eager hands, revealing the power of his desire for her.

Now Dalton lost some of the slow control he'd been holding on to. He moved closer, increasing the urgency of his kisses. They were no longer gentle and Bonnie no longer wanted them to be.

She tugged his pants down over his hips and slid her hand behind the waistband of his briefs along his warm, smooth skin. He was tightly muscled everywhere, and her fingertips danced along the hard contours of his body.

She moved her hand to the front and found he was ready for her, a fact that made her tingle hotly right through her core.

"You sure you know what you're doing?" Dalton asked, his voice just a rasp of breath. "Because in about two seconds, I'm not going to be able to stop."

"I already can't," she breathed, then kissed him again.

He was more than willing to comply.

Their tongues moved against each other, mirroring the rhythm that was beginning to synchronize and pound within them.

Dalton unbuttoned Bonnie's shirt with painful deliberation, watching every button come loose as if each one might reveal some great treasure. Finally, he slipped the shirt off of her, holding her gaze with his own, and gave a quick, devilish smile.

Her heart pounded in response.

"You've done this before, Mr. Price."

He shook his head. "Oh, no, Miss Vaness. I've never done *this* before."

Still holding her gaze, he worked his fingers deftly to slip her bra off. He did it in one smooth move, then tossed it aside. By the time he unfastened the top button of her jeans, her need to have him within her was so powerful, she could barely get naked fast enough.

The rough denim slid across her skin, leaving a burning trail of promise.

He put a strong arm around her back and lowered her carefully onto the floor. There was no time for the niceties of moving to the bedroom. The low carpet was cold and rough and had the slightly chemical scent that betrayed its newness.

Dalton's hand moved across her stomach, and lower, to her pelvis, slowing tantalizingly before finally cupping over the part of her that wanted him so desperately.

He paused for only a second, looking into her eyes, before slipping his fingers beneath the thin fabric of her panties and plunging it into her depths. It felt as if he was reaching into her soul. Never had she felt so safe, so *understood,* in her life. Dalton brought her into perfect rhythm, not only with him, but with herself.

Then he took her above it, building a bud of tension deep inside of her that only he could satisfy.

And he did.

Bonnie's fingers clutched at the carpet beneath her as Dalton worked magic on her that she'd never imagined. She closed her eyes and let it happen, watching colors she'd never seen before pass behind her eyelids until gradually her breath came in ragged gasps and she turned her head from side to side. Finally he allowed her release.

With exquisite timing, Dalton moved to lower his weight on her, pressing the breath from her lungs as he began to move against her. She wouldn't have thought it was possible to respond with more heat, but her body did.

Breathless, she opened her mouth and allowed his kisses to deepen, satiating a thirst she had not realized before, while he moved his hands into her hair, holding her tight while he kissed her face, her neck, her lips, her jaw.

Just when she thought she couldn't take any more, he shifted and, in one smooth motion, he entered her.

He was no longer the nineteen-year-old she had held a burning crush for, and she was no longer the timid eighteen-year-old who had lain timidly beneath him, afraid of getting it wrong.

This time, it was right.

But just this once, she told herself, as she soared into ecstasy. After this, it was over.

"We can't do that again."

"No kidding, we did it three times last night." Dalton rolled over in the bed and looked at Bonnie with sleepy blue eyes.

"No, I mean, we can't do it again at all. Ever. It was a huge mistake."

Dalton sat up, his muscular torso spotlighted by a slice of morning light that was cutting through the curtains. "A mistake."

"Not that it wasn't great," she hastened to add. "It was, it was a...great mistake."

He raked his hand through his mussed hair and shook his head, smiling. "I guess that's a compliment. Funny how it doesn't really feel like one."

An awkward silence rose between them and expanded to fill the room.

"It's not like you're looking for a relationship, right?"

He looked at her for a long moment. "No, I wasn't looking for a relationship."

"And you know I *am*. I mean, that was the whole point of your trying to help me with Mark." She didn't add that she hadn't thought about Mark in a romantic way for days.

Dalton gave a dry smile. "That's right, we got off course there last night."

Bonnie swallowed hard. If that was getting off course, then maybe she didn't want to get back on course. Because even though she'd decided quite firmly that it wasn't good for her to fall for chemistry, it was a draw she couldn't deny. And, clearly, she had a very hard time resisting it.

What if she were dating Mark? Would that chemical attraction develop? If it didn't, would it be enough that he was stable, good-looking and charming? If it wasn't, would she somehow be able to resist physical attraction elsewhere, like with Dalton?

"Is this how you teach seduction now?" she asked, trying to sound lighthearted, but frankly resenting Mark's intrusion on the moment, even though he wasn't really there.

"I can't teach seduction," Dalton said. "That was just a guy talking in a bar. It's not like I have an actual curriculum."

"So you lied." She feigned shock.

"Believe me, you don't need instruction."

"I don't know what I need anymore," she murmured, without looking at him.

"What?"

She looked up. "Never mind." She sat up next to him and drew the sheet up to cover herself, inadvertently pulling it off of him. "Oh! Sorry." She leaned over and hastily moved the sheet over his lap.

He looked at her, bemused. "Suddenly we're strangers?"

"No, I—" That was exactly how she felt. Like

they were strangers who had fallen into bed together after too many drinks in a bar or something. She had let herself in for just the kind of heartbreak she had developed a meticulous plan to avoid. "I just didn't want you to get cold."

He threw the sheet back and stood up, walking to the window. "I'm feeling a chill, that's for sure." He drew the curtain slightly and looked outside.

Light poured into the room, acting as a spotlight on Bonnie's nakedness and vulnerability. She didn't know what to say. He didn't want a relationship, and she didn't want just a bed buddy, so what was the point of prolonging this? "I'd better go home," she said, holding the sheet against her as she got out of the bed.

Dalton shook his head and took a pair of shorts off the back of a chair.

The tension was broken by the unexpected sound of the front door opening.

"Bonnie? Have you seen Daddy?" Elissa's footsteps pounded across the floor and before either Dalton or Bonnie could move, she'd thrown the bedroom door open and burst in.

Chapter Thirteen

"Say what you mean. And mean what you say."
—Dalton Price

"She walked in on you?" Paula asked in disbelief, pouring a cup of coffee and handing it to Bonnie.

"Right in."

"And you were naked?"

"Unless a sheet toga qualifies me as dressed." She sipped the hot liquid, letting it burn down her throat. Anything to take her mind off the horror of a child walking in and instantly realizing what was going on.

"How did she get in?" Paula asked.

"Skeleton key," Bonnie answered, cringing at the memory. "Dalton has a key that opens every apartment in the place. She didn't know what she was doing."

Paula groaned. "Bad, bad, bad. Man, that takes the cake. Was she upset?"

Bonnie shook her head. "It didn't seem like it. She looked surprised that I was there, but she just jumped on the bed and started talking about how her friend got sick so she had to come home early and—" she shrugged "—that sort of thing. There was some description of projectile vomiting."

"Oooh, that'll kill the mood."

"Not as quickly as a child entering unexpectedly and jumping on the bed." Bonnie shuddered at the thought. "I hope to God this doesn't upset her when she has a chance to think about it."

"If it didn't already, why would it later?"

"Because it's just been her and Dalton for so long now. She might get upset and feel threatened or something. That happens all the time. A child with only one parent gets really protective of that parent and doesn't want to share."

Paula scoffed. "Elissa adores you. She's not going to suddenly start resenting you."

"That's for sure," Bonnie said with resolve. "Because this is not going to happen again."

"Why *not?*" Paula was exasperated. "This is so stupid. You're obviously into Dalton, and he's *obviously* into you. So why do you insist on depriving yourself? It's just dumb."

"No, it's not. I'm trying to be mature about this kind of thing for once in my life." Bonnie got up and walked to the coffeemaker to pour herself another cup. "I've spent too many days and weeks of my life pining for a guy who won't call. In fact, I've spent too many days and weeks of my life pining for *Dalton* when *he* wouldn't call. I can't give myself to someone and let them use me until they're finished, then cast me aside. I'm too old to sit in my apartment drowning my sorrows in ice cream and sad songs." She was vehement. "I'm too old to live for the pleasure of the moment without taking into consideration how it will affect me later."

Paula listened, her eyes slowly filling with tears. "I understand. You're right." She sniffed and swiped her hand across her eyes. "But what if Dalton is in it for the long haul this time?"

Bonnie hesitated. "He's had every chance to tell me that." She shook her head and tried to ignore the heartache that threatened. "He's just not there.

Whether it's because of Elissa or because of the way he feels about me…I don't know. It doesn't matter. He's not the guy for me."

"Okay." Paula sighed. "I can't argue with any of that. In fact, I'm the last person in the world who should try, given the mess I've made of my life in the name of lust."

Bonnie set her cup down. "How are you doing?"

Paula shrugged. "I'll be fine, don't worry about me. Look, I refuse to indulge this misguided heartbreak, so if you don't mind, I'd rather just not talk about it at all."

"Okay, but remember you can call me anytime if you do want to talk about it."

"I know." Paula smiled. "Thanks."

"Is it okay to ask how the job search is going?"

"Actually, it's interesting that you ask. I've decided not to work in the city anymore."

"Oh, no." Bonnie's first thought was that she'd no longer have her pal to commute with, but she realized immediately that was selfish, and asked, "What do you have in mind?"

"You're not going to believe this, but I might buy into Crispin's Bakery. Old Mr. Cunliffe has been trying to get me back there for years and I'm thinking now might be the time." Paula had worked in the bakery throughout high school, as the owner, Crispin Cunliffe, was her next-door neighbor. The bakery had actually done quite well for itself and now had a brisk mail-order business for its authentic Scottish baked goods. "So what do you think? Am I crazy to invest my meager savings that way?"

"I think it's great!" Bonnie exclaimed. "Fantastic! I'm even a little jealous."

Paula looked pleased. "Yeah?"

"Are you kidding? You get to sleep in, work in town, have a vested interest in your work, and spend the day cooking and eating. What's to think about?"

"You're right." Paula smiled with genuine pleasure for the first time that morning. "I'm going to do it." She nodded. "And speaking of cooking, my invitation for Thanksgiving still stands if your plans have changed."

Bonnie shook her head. "Thanks, but for Elissa's sake, I have to go through with it here. I can't cancel plans with her the same week she finds me naked in her father's bedroom. *Wrong* message."

"You're right. Just go, get it over with fast, and try and stay as far away from Dalton as you can."

In an apartment that was roughly 950 square feet, it wasn't easy staying far away from Dalton. In fact, even though she did much of the prep work at home in advance, Bonnie still had to spend quite a lot of time in his tiny kitchen, which meant that Dalton spent much of the time so close that she could feel the heat of his body.

"You don't have to hover over me, you know," Bonnie said, kind of hoping, despite herself, that he'd stay. "You can just go watch football like every other man in America."

"Trying to get rid of me?"

"Yes."

"It's not that easy." He scraped a bar stool across the floor and sat down a couple of feet away from her. "You're much more interesting than football."

She worked at the counter and spoke without looking at him. "I bet you say that to all the girls."

"Nope. Most girls come after the Giants. Some even come after the Jets."

She slipped a sidelong glance at him. "How about the Yankees?"

"Nah, forget it." He laughed. "No sex in the spring at all. But for you? I'd make an exception."

She rolled her eyes, not at his words but at the way her heart tripped in response to them. "Please."

He moved closer and looked over her shoulder. "What's that you're doing?"

The tone of his voice, his proximity to her, *something* sent a thrill tickling down her spine. So she concentrated on pressing garlic into the pan. "Making stuffing."

"I thought it came in a box."

"It comes in a box for lazy people."

He looked impressed. "You're really good at this, aren't you?"

She laughed. "My grandmother insisted I should be able to cook. I think that, like you, she thought it was the best way to get a man."

"You got good family." He said it in a matter-of-fact way, but still it gave Bonnie a little chill. Everyone knew Dalton's father was an abusive drunk until he died their junior year in high school. Dalton's mom, probably as a result, was a quivering wallflower who never stood up for herself or her child. She'd moved to Florida to be with her sister years ago, and Bonnie had barely thought of her since. His background was one reason she admired his parenting so much. This apple had definitely, and fortunately, fallen far from the tree. In fact, it wasn't even in the orchard.

"You should be proud of yourself, Dalton," she said, turning to face him. "You're a really good dad."

"I hope so." He didn't look so sure. "That's one area where I've got no room to fail."

"There's no way you could. Elissa is a wonderful kid." Bonnie spoke with her whole heart. She really adored the child. "In fact, I think she's happier than any kid I've ever known. She's lucky to be so close to her father. Try not to let your own past haunt you." She could have hit herself. Here she was, telling him not to let his past haunt him when she had *just* gotten finished bleeding over a past relationship. One that wasn't nearly as important, on balance, as the parental relationship. Before he could call her on it, she smiled and said, "I know, I know, physician heal thyself."

"I wasn't going to say that," he said softly, looking into her eyes. "It's good advice. It actually means a lot to me that you think Elissa's doing okay. Coming from a family like yours, I'd say you know a thing or two about it."

She smiled. "She's doing great."

Their eyes met and held for a moment.

"So…" Without moving, he glanced at the counter by her elbow. "What's that you're throwing together? Some kind of sauce?" His eyes took her in and she felt for a moment like he'd drawn some resolve out of her. The resolve to resist him.

Her breath was shallow. "No, it's a little spice for the sweet potatoes. I don't do marshmallows."

Another moment passed.

"You don't do them?"

"On the sweet potatoes, Dalton. *Or* for whatever body part you're thinking of."

He laughed softly. "I wasn't thinking anything like that."

He didn't move his hand from her back and she didn't pull away from his touch.

Though she knew she should. "You're *always* thinking something like that."

He clucked his tongue against his teeth. "I'm going to have to be more careful if you can read my mind."

Then, almost beyond her control, Bonnie looked at his mouth and felt a longing more insistent than anything she'd ever felt around Mark Ford or any other man.

Why was she so drawn to Dalton?

Every time she was alone with him lately, her personal battle for willpower became more and more intense.

Tonight was no exception.

And when he leaned forward and kissed her, she kissed him right back.

It felt great. He was an expert with his mouth. Always had been. As he moved his lips over hers, gently but insistently, she felt her knees weaken. She shifted her weight to keep from falling down altogether, and he locked his strong arms around her. They leaned back against the kitchen counter, mouth to mouth, chest to chest, pelvis to pelvis....

It would be easy to go too far again, Bonnie thought vaguely. Her mind was like a tiny cartoon angel standing on her shoulder wagging her finger, while her body was the devil on the other side. Much bigger, much louder. Much more persuasive.

And Bonnie *had* always looked better in red than in white.

"Wait." Somehow she managed to put her hand against Dalton's hard, muscled chest and pushed. "We can't do this."

"Yes, we can." He kissed her again.

And *again* she kissed him right back, moving her hands up from his chest to his thick, wavy hair. She sighed into his mouth. She'd thought about this so many times over the years, even while she fought it. Maybe a girl never forgot her first time, or maybe a girl just never forgot Dalton Price. Bonnie couldn't say. All she knew was that he'd been so good that one night had provided fodder for the occasional lapse into fantasy for years. How could she stop this *now?*

Maybe just a few more minutes wouldn't hurt, the devil in stylish red said to her, and she drew him closer still, deepening the kiss. It just felt so good. Maybe she could get him out of her system, just by letting this go on a little longer.

After what seemed both an eternity and no time at all, she gathered her will and drew back.

"Elissa might come in—"

He kept his mouth on hers for one more moment, then drew back, leaving Bonnie feeling a sudden chill. "You're right."

She wanted to crawl right back into his arms, but she didn't. "And other things."

"Of course," he said flatly. "With you, there are always *other things,* aren't there?"

She turned and looked at him. "It's not just me. It's us. I don't know what it is, Dalton, but with us, there's just no…I don't know, there doesn't seem to be a connection."

"You've got to be kidding."

Her face felt warm. "Well, there's a connection, but…I guess what I mean is that there's no follow-through." She returned to the counter and chopped the end of an onion. "Nothing lasting."

"No *relationship*. Just sex. Is that what you're saying?"

"I guess so." She pulled the papery skin off the onion and dropped it in the garbage can.

"Isn't that because you don't want a relationship?"

"I think it's because *you* don't. You know, last time we slept together, well, the first time, you never called again."

"That was *years* ago."

"So? That might make it less relevant today, but it doesn't make it less important to me." Her eyes began to burn. It was the onions, she told herself as she chopped.

"I didn't know it was important to you."

She took a rib of celery and broke off the stalk. "It was. But how would you know? You never talked to me again."

"Do you really want to get into this ancient history?"

She glanced at him. "Yes. I need to."

He studied her without a readable expression. "Okay, I'll bite. How much do you remember about that night?"

Every detail. "Enough."

"Me, too. And as I recall it, everything ended when you said you had to go home."

She was confused. "Is that bad?"

"Not bad." He took a short breath. "But what you said was that you, and I'm quoting now, you 'shouldn't have done that.'"

She scanned her memory. "It was past my curfew.

I was afraid my dad would be up waiting for me and he'd kill us both."

"You 'shouldn't have done that,' you said."

"I *meant* I shouldn't have stayed out so late."

He hesitated. "But you *said* you shouldn't have done *that*. You didn't make any further explanations."

"Okay, so I said that. So what?"

"So I figured you thought you shouldn't have done it. Been with me." He shrugged. "So what would you have done if you were me? Called back for more rejection?"

"I—" She stopped and really thought about it. If he'd said to her that he shouldn't have done that, if he'd expressed any sort of regret at all after they'd just made love, she would have been crushed.

"You...?" He had a point and he knew it.

She sighed. "I don't know."

"Sure you do." He laughed. "You would have figured the girl regretted having anything to do with you. Especially since she was hauling her butt out of there before your heart rate even returned to normal."

"But my curfew—"

"Maybe. But I didn't know that."

"Okay," she said slowly, "but you could have called to find out for sure instead of just making assumptions."

There was a silence during which she could imagine him shrugging it off. "That's the difference between you and me."

"Daddy?"

Bonnie was startled by the child calling from the other room.

"Yeah?" Dalton called back, his eyes still on Bonnie.

Elissa showed up in the doorway to the kitchen. "When's dinner?"

Dalton looked at Bonnie.

She cleared her throat and tried to shake the mood that had taken over the kitchen. "In about forty-five minutes."

Elissa looked from Dalton to Bonnie and back again. "'Kay. I'm going to read in my room. Just call me when dinner's ready."

The child left and Bonnie turned back to Dalton, wide-eyed. "She thinks something's going on between us."

"It is."

"It isn't. Didn't we just establish that?" She looked at him. Blue eyes. Black hair. A perfectly chiseled face, like something made in ancient Greece. And that mouth. Dazzling when he smiled. Sensual when he didn't. He was a hard guy to resist.

"We just established that you're pissed off about

something that happened ten years ago, but other than that…" He shrugged. "I'm not sure we established what's going on with us now."

"Nothing is going on with us now." Somehow it didn't feel right, at this moment, to remind him that what was going on with them now was Dalton trying to help Bonnie win over another guy.

Besides, she couldn't allow anything to be going on with her and Dalton, even if Mark wasn't a factor. Whatever the reason, she'd been hurt by Dalton before. Given her history, sometimes it was all she could do to consider having a relationship again at all, but the idea of having one with someone who had *already* burned her… Once upon a time the optimism of youth—along with some pretty raging hormones—had given her the faith and the foolishness to ignore past hurts. Hope that Dalton would call had burgeoned in her heart far longer than she cared to admit, even to herself. And even if she could understand why he'd been reluctant to call, some part of her still thought he should have called anyway.

Now things were different. Now her body didn't tend to betray her as much. Nowadays, her mind had a lot more say in the matter of who she fell for, and her mind wasn't about to let her go traipsing into an emotionally loaded situation, like falling for Dalton Price.

"Nothing's going on with us now," he repeated.

"Right," she agreed, with a little less certainty than she'd had just a few minutes ago.

"Right." For his part, he sounded certain.

"That's what you want...right?"

"Of course. You too. Right?"

"Sure."

"You're still all about Mike."

She nodded, then realized the mistake and corrected it. "Mark."

He snapped his fingers. "That's right, Mark. Why can't I remember that?"

"I don't know." She forced a laugh. "Can I finish cooking now?"

"Why not?" With a smile, he walked a few steps away, sat down at the counter and picked up the newspaper. "You've already heated things up plenty."

Chapter Fourteen

*"Sometimes what you need is looking you right
in the face and you don't even know it."*

—Fate

"That was the best Thanksgiving turkey I ever had,"
Elissa said with a yawn. She threw herself into Bonnie's arms on the couch and snuggled in. "You're a
great cook."

"The secret is in putting the turkey in salt water
first, just like I showed you," Bonnie said. "You could
have done it yourself. With a little help from your dad

putting it into the oven, that is." She looked at Dalton over Elissa's head.

He shrugged. "I don't know, Bon. Seems like you've got the magic touch when it comes to cooking. If you ever want to quit your big city job and come work for me for a hundred bucks a month, you just say the word."

"Generous of you," Bonnie replied dryly. "But I think I'll keep my job."

He shrugged. "Don't say I didn't offer."

She smiled and leaned her cheek against Elissa's head, drawing in the sweet scent of Johnson's baby shampoo. "Thanks."

Elissa yawned again. "Last year we went to Denny's for Thanksgiving."

"You *did?*" Bonnie looked at Dalton, aghast.

"Wait a minute, I tried to cook dinner myself—"

"He forgot to turn the oven on," Elissa interjected. "The turkey was all white and slimy."

Bonnie looked at Dalton. "Ew."

He nodded. "It was horrible."

Bonnie was saddened that Dalton's attempt to make a traditional dinner for Elissa had failed, and even more sad to picture them sitting at a sterile Formica table at what was only one step above a fast-food restaurant. "That's really sad."

"Daddy ended up going out with our waitress," Elissa added.

Bonnie's pity for Dalton dissolved. "Really."

He gave a wide shrug and an even wider smile. "What can I say? Pitiful is attractive to some women."

Elissa tapped on Bonnie's arm, distracting her from the hot retort she was ready to fire at Dalton. "Bonnie, will you tuck me in?"

"Sure, honey." Bonnie looked to Dalton for confirmation and he nodded.

"I'll take care of the dishes," he told her.

As sexy as he was, offering to do the dishes took it up a notch in Bonnie's book. "Don't forget to turn the faucet on."

"Very funny."

"And open the soap container before turning it upside down."

He gave a good-natured laugh. "Get out of here."

"Okay, then, let's go." Bonnie gently eased the child off her lap and stood up.

She led the sleepy child to the bathroom and supervised tooth brushing and face washing before following her to her room. "Do you want to read a book, or…?" Bonnie was uncertain what to do with a nine-year-old child. Did they still want to have bedtime stories? "Or should we just talk?"

"Let's talk." Elissa threw back the sheets and covers and climbed into her bed, then patted the space next to her for Bonnie.

"Okay." Bonnie sat down and dimmed the light. "What do you want to talk about?"

"You know that movie we watched the other night?" Elissa asked, getting straight to the point. "About the kids getting their parents together?"

"Mmm, hmm." Bonnie stroked Elissa's hair and prayed she wasn't about to ask if Bonnie could help her fix up Dalton with his ex-wife.

"Well…you and my dad used to go out, right?"

Bonnie shrugged in the darkness. "We were friends a long time ago. Why?"

"Were you in love?"

Oh.

That was the question of the decade. Was Bonnie in love with Dalton way back when? It had certainly felt like it at the time. And for several years afterward. And pretty much every time she thought of him, even to this day. "Why do you ask, honey?" she asked Elissa, trying to deflect the question.

"Because I was thinking if you were in love then maybe I could make it like it was your first date again and things would go better this time." She said it like it was a simple and workable plan. Easy, even.

But things of the heart were never so easy. Bonnie knew that well now. Especially where Dalton Price was concerned.

"Oh, sweetie, it's not like that for your dad and me." She gave Elissa a squeeze and kissed the top of her head. "We're just friends, that's all."

Elissa looked up at her in the darkness, and even though the only light came from the hall, Bonnie could see the sharp look of disbelief in her eyes. "Does Daddy know?"

Bonnie couldn't help but give a laugh. "Yes, of course he knows, sweetie. He told me a long time ago that was all he wanted us to be. It's fine."

Elissa shook her head. "I don't know. I think he changed his mind."

Bonnie mussed her hair. "I never should have shown you that silly romantic movie."

"No, I loved it."

Bonnie smiled and shook her head. "I love it, too. Looks like we're both silly romantics."

"That's okay," Elissa said, snuggling deeper under the covers and turning on her side. "It's better than liking football."

Bonnie laughed aloud and decided there would probably be a better time to let Elissa know she liked the New York Giants almost as much as Dalton did.

When the child's breathing grew slow and even, Bonnie carefully and reluctantly extracted herself from the bed and made her way, blinking at the light, back into the hall.

"She asleep?" Dalton asked, swabbing the counter with a bar rag.

Bonnie nodded. "Tryptophan works its magic again. If they could put Thanksgiving turkey in pill form, no one would have insomnia."

Dalton gave a broad smile and agreed. "I've been wanting to go lie down myself." A moment passed. "Want to come?"

"I...think I'd better go home." Bonnie's heart hammered in her chest as she spoke, even though she knew Dalton was probably just being smart with her. "You've got enough to be thankful for tonight, what with that little girl in the other room." She gave what was meant to be a sassy smile. "I don't want to overwhelm you."

"You take the cake, you know that?" He answered with what could only be described as a pirate's smile, and Bonnie felt her breath catch in her throat. "But I'll keep the pie, if it's all the same to you."

"Be my guest."

"So...you got plans for Christmas?"

It was a month away, and, no, she had none. "Why? You looking for a caterer again?"

"I need to use my remaining dinners wisely."

"I think holidays count for at least double."

He nodded. "Probably so. You really should have laid that rule down when we started."

"Well, I'm laying it down now. Jeez, a girl's really got to be on her toes with you, Dalton."

He leveled his gaze on her like the red sights of a hunting gun. "Why is that?" He took a step toward her and looked down at her in a way that made her breath go shallow.

"Because you always seem to get your way."

"Not always," he said softly.

Her heart fluttered. "Name me one time you didn't get what you wanted."

He hesitated. For a long time. Then, his voice barely above a whisper, he said, "I really wanted a BB gun when I was a kid, but my father wouldn't let me have one."

She had to laugh, despite the strange letdown of his revelation. "On behalf of all of the citizens of Tappen, I'd like to thank your dad for that."

And with that, the moment was over.

"It's getting late," Bonnie said, with no actual idea what time it was.

"Yeah," Dalton agreed.

"I'd better go." She looked into his eyes.

"You don't have to."

Oh, yes, she did. Otherwise, she might throw herself at him. "I think I left the water running."

He took a step closer. "That's okay, I pay the water bills."

"It might have been the heat, then."

He looked her over. "You definitely turned the heat on."

She swallowed hard, and tried to think of something—anything—other than his eyes. And his mouth. And his—

"So if you want to turn it off, you'd better go now."

She nodded, barely looking at him as she made her way to the door. "I think that's best." She stopped and turned back. "Good night, Dalton."

The Monday night following Thanksgiving was Bonnie's office holiday party. A few weeks ago she'd been looking forward to it as the time she might finally get to have her moment with Mark, but she wasn't thinking so much about Mark lately.

In fact, as she spent an hour getting ready, she found herself thinking more about concocting a reason to stop at Dalton's on her way out—once she was all dressed up.

Which was how she finally settled on a red sleeveless cocktail dress that fit like a dream in the waist, then fell into a flattering pencil skirt. She looked a little like a gangster's moll in it, but she knew it looked good from behind so she chose it anyway.

She toyed with excuses for stopping at Dalton's all the way down to his apartment but when she knocked on the door, all she could think of was to ask him to look for a mouse in her apartment. It was lame but it was the best she could come up with.

As it turned out, she didn't need any excuse at all. When Elissa opened the door, she told Bonnie that her father went out to meet with some woman.

As Bonnie got to the bottom of the stairs she was startled by the sound of a low whistle.

"You are *smokin'* in that dress," Dalton said.

Bonnie's heart flipped, probably from the shock of running into someone in the empty hall. "Thanks, Dalton."

"Where are you off to?" he asked.

"Holiday party at work."

"Well, you are *not* taking public transportation looking like that," Dalton said, taking his keys out of his pocket. "It's just not safe. Let me give you a ride."

"Oh, no, you don't have to do that. I've got a cab coming."

"You sure? I'm on my way out anyway."

"Oh. You are? Where to?" She tried to sound light, but didn't quite make it.

"I've got a late conference at the school with one of Elissa's teachers."

Bonnie looked at her watch. "Awfully late. It's almost six." She pictured a pretty young teacher, with luscious chestnut hair piled atop her head in a tousled bun.

"Yeah, she's had conferences all day. I asked for the last one so I could get Elissa fed and settled before I go."

"Hm." In her mind's eye now, Bonnie could see Dalton removing a pin from that bun, and the woman's hair tumbling down around her shoulders. It was like a scene from a steamy movie. "So I guess tonight's the night."

"Yeah." He smiled. "This is your chance, right?"

"Chance?"

"With Mark. Isn't that what you meant about tonight?"

It hadn't been at all, of course, she'd just been babbling, but she couldn't let him know that. She forced her thoughts from Dalton and the teacher to Mark. "Yes. That's what I was thinking. We'll be in the office, but maybe we can make it…you know…personal."

"Sweetheart, if you're dressed like that, it doesn't matter *where* you are." He gave a shake of his head. "This is your big night."

If she'd imagined, even for a moment, that Dalton wanted her for himself, this clinched it. He didn't. "You think so? For me and Mark?"

"I know it." He looked her up and down. "If he doesn't make a move, he's an even bigger idiot than I thought."

"All right, what do you suggest I do?" She might as well get her money's worth from him. He was supposed to teach her how to seduce a man. It was never part of the deal that *he'd* be the man she seduced, so she had no business feeling like she'd lost something.

Three heartbeats passed between them.

"You know what you should do?" Dalton asked at last. "You should just tell him the truth. No one ever tells the truth anymore."

"The truth." It was an idea that had never occurred to her. "What, that I want him?"

Dalton's jaw tightened for a moment, but the quick smile he gave dissolved any thoughts she had that he might be jealous. "Yes. Tell him just that. You want the guy? Go get him. Stop messing around with games."

"Because if you want to be with someone, you should just tell them that," Bonnie reiterated carefully. "That's your philosophy."

He nodded once. "That's my philosophy. Tell the truth. No more BS."

She took a long, strained breath. "Okay, then. I'll try it."

They looked at each other in silence for a moment.

Dalton was the one to speak first. "So, uh, if you're sure you don't want a ride...?"

"No, thanks." As if on cue, a yellow cab pulled up in front of the lobby door. "My chariot is here now." She headed for the door and Dalton opened it for her. "Good luck with your meeting tonight," she said as she passed.

"You too," he said, practically stopping her with the intensity of his gaze. "Go get him."

Chapter Fifteen

"Lay your cards on the table. Before it's too late."

—Dalton Price

"Go get him, go get him, go get him," Bonnie chanted in her head, more determined than ever to stop thinking about Dalton and just go out with Mark. Sure, maybe he was a little bit dull, but that was a *good* thing, wasn't it? It meant that he was less likely to get bored with her and go looking for someone else.

As soon as she walked into the office, she saw him—as if in a movie—standing directly opposite her, a sea of people between them. With one short, bolstering breath she went toward him, exchanging small smiles and simple words with her co-workers until she got to him.

He looked up just as Don Piles was finishing a joke about a duck in a bar, and his eyes lit upon her.

"Bonnie." He sounded surprised. "You look stunning."

"Thank you." She gave her most confident smile. "So do you."

"Could you excuse us, Don? Bonnie and I need to talk about…something." He didn't wait for an answer, but smoothly slipped his arm in hers and led her down the back hall. "Thanks for saving me from any more of Don's duck jokes. He must have a hundred of them."

Bonnie smiled, but she didn't feel particularly happy. Mark was finally leading her off to be alone with him and all she could think about was the way Dalton had looked when she had left. "That could come in handy if we get the Pernox Boot account."

Mark laughed, exhibiting teeth so even and white they looked fake. But they weren't, of course. They were just perfect.

Just like Mark himself.

"I put some champagne aside in my office," he said, rounding the corner with her. "Care for a glass?"

"Sure." This was it. Mark Ford was offering her a glass of champagne in his office, alone, after hours. This was the moment she'd been waiting for.

Any minute now, she'd probably be really happy.

He opened the door and ushered her in, closing it with a soft click behind them. She noticed he locked it, too.

Good, she thought, with a strange trepidation tightening in her stomach.

He poured champagne neatly into two elegant flutes and handed one to her.

Instead of concentrating on his handsomeness in this romantic moment, all she could think about was the fact that the guy had champagne flutes in his office. Did he keep them there all the time? Or had he put them there specifically in preparation for tonight? And, if it was the latter, was he planning all along to bring Bonnie back here or was she just the first one to strike his fancy?

"To you," he said, clinking his crystal glass against hers. "Here's to happy holidays and new things to come." He gave a wink and took a sip of champagne.

She sipped too. It was toasty and bright, obviously French and undoubtedly expensive. She continued to be surprised by him, even now.

"I've been hoping to have an opportunity like this with you for some time now," he said to her.

"Have you?" she asked, more curious than excited.

"Weeks," he said with a somber nod. "I've fought against my feeling that co-workers shouldn't get involved, but in your case I just have to make an exception." He set his glass down—on his ink blotter, she noticed, not on the bare wood—then took hers from her hand and set it next to his. "We've got something special between us. I think you feel it, too."

It was on the tip of her tongue to ask if this was a serious line, and if it had ever worked on a woman before, but she didn't get the chance. Before she could say a word, he crushed his mouth onto hers in a long, hard kiss.

He didn't move a muscle. Not his mouth, not his arms. Nothing.

All at once Bonnie realized that she felt nothing for this man. Her heartbeat, if anything, had slowed to a lulled, relaxed state. There was no question of things going further with Mark, there just wasn't a chance. Everything Paula had said to her was true; she *needed* passion, even if it did represent emotional risk. She'd rather be alone than living a lie with a man who made her feel like watching TV or playing solitaire when he kissed her.

Bonnie waited a moment, curious to see if he was planning some great move, but it didn't happen. It was as if he was stuck. He just stood there, his mouth pressed to hers like he was trying to mash her lips flat.

She laughed.

She just couldn't help it.

That got him moving. He backed up, a look of surprise in his eyes. "What's so funny?" he asked sharply.

She realized immediately that her laughing had embarrassed him, so she tried to smooth over his ego. "You had me going for a minute there, Mark. Phew." She drew a hand across her forehead. "Wow, you could really turn a girl's head. Even a girl like me, who's…engaged."

He glanced at her bare left hand. "Engaged?"

She followed his gaze. "Yes. Well, we haven't picked out the ring yet because he's giving me his grandmother's and it's being sized." She remembered hearing that if you're going to tell a lie you should give it as many details as possible so it will sound true. "She was a very small woman. Almost weirdly small, actually." She shook her head, as if musing over her imaginary fiancé's tiny grandmother. "Anyway, if he found out that we just…well, he'd be so upset."

"Who are you engaged to?"

"Uh. You remember—" she searched her mind and found her answer immediately "—Dalton? Guy I knew from school? You met in the lobby downstairs."

"Oh, yes. Him?"

"Yes." She nodded. "I just hope he's not carrying the tiny grandmother's genes, you know?"

Mark gave an awkward smile. "I'm really sorry to have…I thought you were available…"

"I've tried to keep my personal life out of the office." Where was this coming from? She *hated* lying. But, in this case, it was better than the truth. "Anyway, I know you were just trying to goad it out of me, and you did." She pointed a finger at him. "You're a sneaky one."

He gave another self-conscious smile, then said, "You got me. I was just kidding around. But, seriously, can I ask you something?"

Oh, no. "Sure, what is it?"

"That girl who's in charge of the accounting department."

"Debra?"

He snapped his fingers. "Debra. Do you know if *she's* seeing anyone?"

It had been almost twenty years since Dalton had walked through the doors of Tappen Elementary

School, but the smell reminded him immediately of how much he'd hated it there.

That and the fact that he had to meet with a teacher about a problem.

But in this case, the teacher was Elissa's, not his. And Mrs. Zaharis was a lot nicer than the teachers he remembered from his days.

"Mr. Price, let me get right to the point, and please forgive me if I'm too blunt. Are you getting married?"

He nearly choked. "Married? No. Why?"

She gave a sad shake of her head. "That's what I thought. Elissa is projecting, talking about you getting married and giving her a new mother. I think she's really feeling the lack of her own mother during the holidays."

"She's never said anything like that."

"Children communicate in many ways other than talking."

He knew that. He was her father, for Pete's sake. Elissa had been acting perfectly normal. "Did she have anyone in particular in mind that I'm supposed to be marrying?"

"She talks about a woman named Bonnie. Is there—" Mrs. Zaharis hesitated "—a Bonnie in your life?"

He thought about Bonnie, then about Bonnie and Mark. Was there a Bonnie in his life? Not in any real sense.

He wished there was. In a way, he'd had Bonnie in his life since second grade and he didn't like the idea that she'd moved on to someone else's life, to snipe at someone else instead of him for the rest of eternity.

He'd gotten kind of used to it.

Even gotten to kind of like it.

"Not really. Just a neighbor."

"As I suspected. She's got it in her head that she wants a mother, so she's chosen someone convenient." Mrs. Zaharis gave a sympathetic smile. "It happens all the time."

Dalton shrugged. "So I'll just tell her she's got the wrong idea. That should take care of it, right?"

"Mr. Price, there are child education specialists who would tell you to coax it out of her and let her work it out in her own mind, at her own pace, but I am not one of them. I'm with you on this one. I say just tell her the truth, flat out, and then make sure that she sees nothing that gives her the impression that you aren't being sincere." She leaned forward. "In other words, if this Bonnie is an attractive neighbor with whom you sometimes linger at the mailbox, cut that behavior out. Be curt and businesslike." She leaned back again. "Elissa will see that and get the idea that this woman is not a significant part of your life."

Dalton frowned. "Are you saying I shouldn't even be friendly with her?"

Mrs. Zaharis tightened her lips and shook her head. "Cordial, but nothing beyond that. Believe me, it's the only way."

As soon as Bonnie got home that night, removed her impractical shoes and dropped, exhausted, onto her sofa, there was a knock on the door.

"Who is it?" she called, expecting it to be Paula.

"Dalton."

Her hand went up reflexively to fix her hair before she said, "Come on in, you've got a key."

The door opened. "I don't need a key. Like a fool, you always leave the door unlocked."

She smiled. It was so good to see him, she could have just sighed. "But like a dad, you always leave the security lock on in the lobby, so I don't *need* to lock my door. Unless I want to keep you out." She realized when the words were out that it could be taken as an implication that she didn't want to keep him out, but she didn't correct herself. "So what's up? How was your meeting?"

"Actually, it didn't go as easily as I thought it would."

"No?" So the buxom young teacher of her imagination had rebuffed him? That was good.

"We need to talk." He gestured at the sofa. "Can I sit down for a minute?"

"Of course." She straightened, thrown by his tone. "Is there some way I can help?"

"Yes. As a matter of fact, there is." He pinched the bridge of his nose for a moment, then looked at her soberly. "I know this is going to sound crazy, but Elissa's gotten some pretty wild ideas about you and me."

"What kind of ideas?"

"She's been telling everyone that we're getting married. That you're going to be her new mother."

"Oh." Bonnie was touched. "That's so sweet."

Dalton's eyes were dark. "According to her teacher, it's unhealthy. She suggests we keep some distance between us."

"We—you and me?"

He nodded.

Her heart sank. "Is that what you want?"

"It doesn't matter what I want. Look, this has been fun, and the meals have been great, but you don't need to hang around me. You've got all the tools to go out and get your man, you always did. It was just…I don't know, I guess I was looking to spend time with you for my own selfish reasons."

"And now…?" she asked, with a modicum of hope.

"Now I know that's a bad idea."

A lump of emotion worked its way into Bonnie's throat. "I'm sorry to hear that."

"It's not like we have to pretend we don't know each other or anything," he said, looking at her steadily. "It's just that—" he shrugged "—since our relationship is *not* what Elissa thinks it is, it would be unfair to keep spending so much time together and with her because it just gets her hopes up."

And Bonnie's too, she realized now. "I understand," she said, with utter sincerity.

"I knew you would." Dalton stood.

She stood as well.

"Thanks a lot, Bon," he said, looking at her, then glancing away quickly. He headed for the door. "By the way—" he stopped and turned back to her "—how was the party? Did you get what you wanted?"

"Almost," she said with a smile. "It was close."

"Well, keep trying. You can't miss."

"Thanks." She stood by the door and watched him go down the hall. "Good night, Dalton."

"Night," he answered, without looking back.

* * *

"So that's just it? Good night?" Paula squeezed pastry cream into puff pastry and looked at Bonnie. "Girl, you are blowing this big time."

"Blowing what?" Bonnie reached out and took a finger full of the cream before Paula slapped her hand away.

"Blowing things with Dalton." She hurled the cream puff at Bonnie. "Here. Eat this, I can't sell it now that you've touched it."

Bonnie took the cream puff gladly and bit into it. It was perfect. An airy pastry with smooth, light, vanilla cream in the center. "This is the best thing I've ever had," she told Paula. "Even better than Crispin's own." And it was a good thing, too, because she was probably going to have to enjoy this instead of sex for the rest of her life.

"Don't change the subject," Paula said, flushing with pride and handing Bonnie another. "Back to you and Dalton."

"There *is* no me and Dalton. You have to face that. If *I* have to face it, then you definitely have to face it."

"Nope." Paula shook her head. "Sorry, I can't give up. He loves you and you love him. It's always been that way and it's about damn time you realized it."

Bonnie's heart broke to hear Paula say that. "He's

had every chance to say he feels something, but he hasn't. I don't want a guy by default, or just for the occasional roll in the hay, I want a guy who wants me so badly he'll do *anything* to win me over."

"Anything, huh? Like wearing clothes like yours and breathing with you?"

"At least I was *trying*. And that was for a guy I didn't even love. If a guy loves me he should do that and more."

"He told you why he didn't."

"Oh, please." She'd already considered that. "This stuff about *guessing* I didn't want to hear from him is just so—so—"

"So similar to what you're doing with him now?"

Bonnie leveled a gaze on Paula. "So namby-pamby."

"Not like that hunka hunka burning love, Mark Bored, you spent months trying to talk yourself into."

Bonnie took a thoughtful bite of cream puff. "Only at the end. In the beginning I was really interested in him, but now…" She shrugged. "He's just so…"

"Namby-pamby."

Bonnie sighed. "I'm afraid so. When he kissed me, it was exactly like one of those 1940s movie kisses. All hard and smashed against me. No passion at all."

"Ew."

"Yeah. Ew."

"Could it be—" Paula moved one tray of finished pastries aside and took down another tray of shells "—that your heart just wasn't in it because there was someone else?"

Bonnie raised a weary brow. "Someone like Dalton?"

"You said it, not me."

Bonnie sighed. "Well, the kiss would have been *ew* anyway, but, yes, I'll admit it. I was starting to have feelings for Dalton." She reached out for another lick of cream.

Paula grabbed her wrist. "Then tell him. You have to tell him. God, Bonnie, he loves you, I just know he does. It's all over his face every time he's around you." She let go of Bonnie. "Just like it's all over yours."

Tears filled Bonnie's eyes. "Is it?"

"Yes, honey. It really is." Paula handed her a third cream puff.

Bonnie ate it in one bite and asked, mouth full, "Don't you think it's too late?"

"It's never too late. Tell him the truth."

"That's weird. That's just what he told me the other night. To go tell Mark the truth."

"Well, he may have said Mark but he was talking

about himself. And if you don't go talk to him right now I'm going to call him myself and tell him everything."

"You wouldn't dare!"

"Oh, yeah?" Paula asked fiercely. "Try me."

Something about the look in Paula's eye told Bonnie she was not bluffing this time.

"You're not kidding, are you?" Bonnie asked.

Paula shook her head. "I figure at least one of us should have a happy ending."

Bonnie took a deep breath. She had nothing to lose by trying. If she opened up to Dalton and he didn't want anything more to do with her, she'd be no worse off than she was now. Maybe her pride would be hurt for a little while, but that was no reason to keep this in anymore. "Okay," she said, firmly. "I'm going to do it."

"Way to go!"

"This may be a huge mistake."

"Or possibly the best move of your life. You never know until you try."

Bonnie gave a dry smile. "Easy for you to say." She pushed off the counter and started to leave. "Wish me luck."

"Wait. Here." Paula handed Bonnie an overflowing cream puff. "Take this for courage. You're gonna need it."

Chapter Sixteen

"Sometimes you've just got to take a chance on telling someone the truth about how you feel. It might be worth it."

—Bonnie Vaness

Everywhere she went in the building, Bonnie ran into someone, but for once it was never Dalton.

Nelly Malone was in the lobby, wrestling her key into the mailbox lock.

"Have you seen Dalton, Mrs. Malone?" Bonnie asked her.

"Ah, yes," the older woman said. "Many times."

Bonnie swallowed her frustration. "Do you know where he is right now?"

Nelly Malone appeared to consider this carefully, before nodding and saying, "No, I don't."

Puzzled, Bonnie left and went to his apartment for the second time. She knocked and knocked, then waited by the door, half wondering if he knew it was her and simply wasn't answering.

It wasn't until Cindy Payne came into the hall from the stairwell, struggling with little Liam and his stroller, that she realized how embarrassing it was to be just standing there.

She rushed to help Cindy with the stroller.

"Thanks," Cindy said, settling the baby onto her ample hip. "It never occurred to me how important elevators were until I moved in here. Thank goodness Dalton's going to fix up the one in the back."

"There's an elevator in the back?" Bonnie asked, amazed.

Cindy laughed. "Don't worry, it's not that you didn't see it. It's been walled in. Dalton showed it to me this morning. It's a really cool old birdcage-style elevator."

Bonnie sighed. She'd been missing so much, so many things that were right in front of her. What a lot of time she'd wasted, looking down her planned-out future instead of looking at everything around her now.

"Have you seen Dalton today?" she asked Cindy, then, realizing Cindy had just said she had, amended, "I mean, do you know where he is now?"

Concern crossed Cindy's brow. "Is everything all right?"

"Fine. I just need to talk to him."

"Well, actually I did just see him."

Bonnie sighed with relief. "Where?"

"He's on the roof." Cindy pointed upward. "He called out to Liam and me as we came down the block."

"On the roof?" Bonnie thought about it for a moment. There was only one stairwell in the building, so that had to be the way up, though she'd never gone beyond her own floor. "Thanks," she said, turning toward the stairwell. "I owe you one."

She opened the heavy door to the stairs and flipped the light switch on. The bulb was out so the corridor remained in darkness. She made her way up, hoping it would become obvious when and if she came to the roof.

It was. A crack of light shone under the door and when Bonnie got to it, she saw that it had been propped open by a small rock. She opened the door carefully and went out.

Dalton was hammering a piece of aluminum sheet metal in place when she came up behind him.

"Dalton?"

He jumped and cursed so loudly she was pretty sure the people in the city probably heard it. "Jeez, Bonnie, what are you doing, trying to kill me?"

She gave an apologetic smile. "No, believe it or not."

He glanced dubiously over the edge of the building. "That could have been ugly."

"Yeah, well, it still could be."

He looked back at her. "What are you talking about?" His face was smudged with blackened soot, and his hair was a perfectly tousled mess. His eyes were bright blue in his tanned face, and Bonnie thought she had never seen a more attractive man.

"Well, you know how you told me to tell the guy the truth? About how I feel about him?"

He ran the back of his hand across his forehead. "Yeah. Did you do that?"

"I'm trying."

"Look, Bonnie, I really don't have it in me to keep coaching you through this. You can have any guy in the world that you want, and you've got better tools for it than anyone. You don't need someone telling you what to do."

"But you already did." Her face felt warm. "You

told me to tell him the truth, and I think that's really good advice, but I'm finding it really hard."

Dalton looked at her. "Why?"

"Because I don't think he's expecting to hear it from me," she said carefully. "And I'm not sure what he'll say."

"If he's even half a man he'll say 'marry me and I'll give you the world.'"

Bonnie's breath caught in her chest. Was he just being nice or was that really how he thought a guy should feel for her? "Okay, so…I'm telling him."

"Good for you." Dalton turned back to his hammering. "Let me know how it goes."

She laughed quietly to herself and walked up behind him, putting her hand on his shoulder.

He turned back to face her, confusion darkening his expression. "What's going on?"

"I *said* I'm telling him how I feel," Bonnie said quietly. "Or at least I'm trying to. It's not Mark, Dalton. He's not the one I'm in love with."

Dalton stood slowly, holding her with his gaze until he was looking down into her eyes. "Tell the truth. And fast before I get my heart set on misunderstanding you."

She took a quavering breath. "It's you, Dalton. It's always been you." She shrugged, her face heating to pink. "I'm in love with you."

"You are."

She nodded, staring at the pebbly surface of the rooftop.

"You're sure."

She nodded again, then looked into his eyes. "I tried to follow my head but my heart just kept getting in the way. Now I think…" Emotion caught in her throat. "Now I think they finally agree."

"Finally," Dalton repeated, taking her into his arms. *"Finally!"* His voice echoed off the ancient brick buildings around them. "Bonnie Vaness, do you have any idea how long I've wanted to hear this from you?"

She shook her head. "Until this moment I wasn't sure you wanted to hear it from me at all."

He laughed, then captured her mouth with his in a long, deep kiss. "You can be pretty dumb sometimes, you know?"

"You've told me that. Numerous times since we were kids."

"It's never been more true. How could you not know how I felt about you?"

"Well, for one thing, you never told me," she began.

"Not in so many words, maybe, but—"

"And for another thing, you told me there was someone else you were interested in."

He frowned. "Someone else?"

"Yes, when we were talking about your love life, or whatever you'd reveal about it, and I asked you if there was someone you were attracted to you said there was someone. And that it was someone I didn't know."

"Ah." His expression cleared. "Yeah. That was you." He cupped his hand on her face and kissed her again. "I had a hunch you didn't really want Mike—"

"Mark."

"—and that you'd figure out there was someone better for you out there."

She smiled. "Are you sure you're better for me than he is?"

"Damn sure." He kissed her again, the wind blowing in spirals around them, but they were as solid together as stone.

It had to be a good omen.

"Bonnie," Dalton said, between kisses.

"Mmmmm?" She didn't want to stop. She didn't ever want to stop.

"Bonnie," he said again, drawing back slightly. "We've got to do this right this time. We've got to make it official."

"Official? What, do you want to take an ad out in the newspaper announcing that we're together?"

"As a matter of fact, that's exactly what I want to do. In the wedding announcements. Next week."

She gasped. "Dalton—"

He knelt on one knee before her and took her hands in his. "Bonnie, I have waited almost all of my life for this and I'm not wasting any more time. Will you do me the honor of spending your life with me, putting up with me and Elissa and anyone else who might come along?" He smiled, the very smile that had always made her heart trip. "Will you marry me?"

When she had imagined this moment in her life, some faceless man she couldn't quite imagine asking her to spend eternity with him, Bonnie always imagined she would freeze. That she would need to ask for more time to think about it. That she might even need to have a decade-long engagement to get used to the idea.

With Dalton, though, it only took a split second. "Yes," she breathed. "Yes, I will."

He stood up. "You've made me the happiest man in the universe."

"You ain't seen nothin' yet."

He smiled. "I'm sorry I don't have the ring ready, but I didn't know this was going to be happening today, obviously."

"I don't need a ring, Dalton. Honestly."

"Look, you gotta have a ring. We could go get one, but my grandmother left one to me that I think was supposed to be used for this purpose someday."

Bonnie looked at him in shock. "Your grandmother?"

He nodded. "It's downstairs. We can get it sized this week."

She couldn't believe the coincidence. "I never met your grandmother, was she…" She swallowed. She'd never had any psychic episodes before and she wasn't sure what to make of this. "Was she a very small woman? Very thin?"

Dalton burst out laughing. "Big as a house. You could probably use the ring as a bracelet right now. Why?"

"Because I told—" She stopped. She didn't want to think about another man right now, especially Mark Ford. She never wanted to think of anyone but Dalton again. "Never mind. I'll tell you the whole long story someday. You can give me a Cracker Jack ring and I'll be happy with it."

He put an arm around her, the wind blowing wildly around them. "I'm gonna give you the world." He gestured with his free arm. "Or at least all of this."

"All I need is you," Bonnie said, her eyes focused

solely on him. "You and Elissa. That's my formula for happily ever after."

"Then you got it, Bonnie Vaness. Forever after."

Epilogue

"Results not typical."
                    —Leticia Bancroft's publisher

"I watched their grandparents get married right in this very spot."

"You did not. Mamie Price couldn't stand you. She thought you were after her husband."

"I was here nevertheless. Edward invited me himself."

"Hrumph."

"He *did*."

The talk around the former Lithuanian Club of Tappen, New Jersey, was all about the weddings that had taken place there before: those of Bonnie's parents and grandparents, and of Dalton's parents, grandparents, and great-grandparents. There were several guests who had attended all of those weddings.

"Mrs. Pringle told me my great-grandmother looked just like me on her wedding day," Bonnie whispered to Dalton as they stood in the traditional receiving line, greeting old friends.

"No offense, but I've seen your great-grandmother and—" Dalton gave her a kiss on the cheek "—she couldn't hold a candle to you."

"Not now, maybe—"

"You're an idiot." Dalton kissed her again. "And I love you. More than you can imagine."

Bonnie turned and looked into the blue eyes that had set her heart pounding for so many years now. She almost couldn't believe that she made him feel the same way he made her feel. "Yeah?"

He touched his fingertip to her nose. "Yeah. Will you marry me?"

"Can't. Sorry." She held up her left hand and wiggled her fingers. "I'm already married. You just missed."

"Bad luck." Dalton took her hand in his and drew

it down to his side. "Hello, Mrs. Perry. We're glad you could make it."

Their second-grade teacher looked from Dalton to Bonnie and back again. "He turned out better looking than I thought he would," she said to Bonnie.

Bonnie smiled and squeezed Dalton's hand in the folds of her skirt. "Aw, come on, Mrs. Perry, I know he was your favorite."

Mrs. Perry broke into a wide grin. "Maybe he was, but he was a rascal then, and I'm sure he's a rascal now."

Bonnie smiled at her husband of one hour. "I'm sure that's true. But at least he's *my* rascal."

"I always knew he would be," the wizened old woman said with a crooked-toothed smile. "The way he teased you, it was impossible to miss how much he adored you."

Bonnie raised her eyebrows and looked at Dalton. "Is that so?"

"If you can't believe the woman who taught you to read, who can you believe?" he asked with a smile.

"Don't listen to her," Maura Tierney, Bonnie and Dalton's sixth-grade music teacher, said, pushing Mrs. Perry aside good-naturedly. "She's a crank."

"I'm not a crank!" Mrs. Perry objected.

"She's a crank," Maura repeated with a knowing

wink. "I've known her for thirty years and she's been a crank the whole time. But she's right about you two."

Mrs. Perry gave a satisfied *hrumph.*

"You two always had some magic between you. I'm just glad you *finally* figured it out." She gave Bonnie a kiss on the cheek, then did the same with Dalton. "Congratulations, kiddo," she said to him. "You got the sweetest girl who ever went to Tappen Junior High School."

"I know it," Dalton said.

The older women moved along, and Bonnie looked at Dalton. "I can't believe those two even made it here today. I wasn't sure they'd remember us."

"Why wouldn't they?" Ignoring the people approaching in the receiving line, Dalton took his new wife's hands in his and gave her a quick but meaningful kiss. "You are unforgettable," he told her.

She beamed, warm under his gaze. "I don't know about that, but you're not going to have to test that ever again. We won't be apart for longer than a workday, and if you forget me that quickly you're in big trouble."

He slipped his hands up her arms and drew her close, whispering in her ear, "Even if you were gone for a hundred years, I wouldn't forget you. I never did, and I never could. Now get back to your wedding guests and tell them goodbye so we can go home and I can show you just how much you mean to me."

"Get a room, you two," Paula whispered next to Bonnie. She was the maid of honor and the unofficial director of the wedding day. "And I mean it. It's time for you to leave. Go on out now and let us throw birdseed at you before we have to throw cold water on you."

Bonnie and Dalton turned back to their guests, ignited by the promise of what was to come later.

They bid their goodbyes, dodged the environmentally correct birdseed that Paula had instructed the guests to throw, and hurried off to the very same 1928 Cadillac that had transported Bonnie's grandparents from their wedding to the Sherborne Hotel in New York City.

As the car chugged its way to the same historic hotel, Dalton turned his attention to Bonnie and said very seriously, "She was right, you know."

"Who?"

"Mrs. Perry. I loved you from the moment I saw you."

"Really?" She flushed with pride. "I thought you were such a jerk. But a cute one." She traced her finger along his jawline and sucked in her breath. "A really cute one."

"Good, 'cause you're stuck with me now."

"And Elissa," Bonnie reminded him, her heart full.

"And Elissa."

"And whoever else might come along."

He went pale. "You're not saying… Are you saying…?"

Bonnie let him sweat for a moment, then shook her head. "But this weekend is a prime opportunity for more little Prices to come along." She raised an eyebrow. "Think you're ready?"

He looked at her, pride and love mingling in his gaze, then he drew her into his arms. "Honey, I was born ready. I can't think of anything I want more than to have kids with you." He kissed her cheek, then her neck. "How soon can we start?"

"Can we get out of the car first?" she asked as the old Caddy entered the Lincoln Tunnel. "Say, fifteen minutes?"

"Maybe," Dalton said, still holding her close. "Just…maybe."

* * * * *